32
MINUTES

ZACH KRAFT

ALSO BY ZACH KRAFT

The Counting Series:

Counting the Ones We Kill

Saving the Ones We Can

Killing the Ones We Can't

32 MINUTES

ZACH KRAFT

The events and characters depicted in this work are fictitious. Any and all similarity to real persons, dead, living, or somewhere in between, is entirely coincidental.

Click or visit:

www.ZachKraft.com

"In a war that begins with an intercontinental ballistic missile, we should consider ourselves lucky. A missile launched from the nearest of the Russian launch sites would come to the president's attention approximately 32 minutes prior to an impact on Washington D.C., plenty of time to coordinate an articulate response..."

Inaugural Memorandum to President-Elect Armstrong
Chairman, Joint Chiefs of Staff

THE BLIP...

It began with a blip.

A tiny red cluster of pixels on a solid LED display buried beneath two-thousand feet of granite.

Like the universe itself, it appeared from nowhere: a quantum spark in space.

One second the region had been black as the void; the next it carried a star, faint in light but brilliant in potential.

The youth at the display leaned in and blinked, wondering if it was a trick of his eye. An afterimage.

A moment before he'd been looking at the much bigger screen in the front of the room. Cable news, talking heads over streaming captions. This was a new beginning, they said as they shivered on the Federal Mall. A day for celebration.

But when the youth blinked again and the red dot remained, he considered that their pronouncements might have been premature.

He picked up the telephone beside his monitor and pressed a button.

"Riley, what can I do for you?" answered a voice, deep with age and experience, much of it underground.

"Sir, I'm picking up a potential LIP on the SEWS."

The line clicked and a moment later the owner of the deep voice was at Riley's back. Together they stared at the box on the right side of Riley's display.

ID: POTENTIAL LAUNCH IN PROGRESS

LAT: 51.5833321
LON: 113.0333387
HEA: 045.892
VEL: 4892 KPH
CKLS: DROVYANAYA, RUSSIAN FEDERATION

Riley hit up a few more displays. "It's validated, sir." He couldn't believe what he'd said. "Heading is high priority."

The man didn't say a word to Riley. He picked up Riley's telephone and spoke from a script he'd read many times before, but never recited.

THE WAY IN. . .

His voice carried a tension she'd never heard before.

"We're not going to make it."

Abigail looked up from her papers to see her husband, staring at a video on his phone. Its speakers gave off a tinny roar: MAYHEM IN MOSCOW. At first she thought he was talking about the news, but then she saw the fidget in his foot. His was a pressing anxiety, not a lingering one. He was worried about something immediate, here. Not something on the other side of the world.

They were late.

She looked at her watch and affected a smile. "You afraid they're going to start the inauguration without us?"

"I'm afraid they'll inaugurate someone else."

Abe released her seatbelt, slid over and pressed her body into Jim's. "I'm not sure that would be a bad thing," she said.

"A little late for doubts, Abe."

A presidency isn't so different from a stint in jail. Utter loss of freedom, of privacy, of dignity—until the people parole you out.

"If you say so," Abe said.

Jim's foot was fidgeting. "I wish your mom could have been here."

"Me too."

"You sure she'll be able to watch?"

"They have TVs in hospitals, Jim."

Abe tried to sound more cavalier than she felt. Truth was, it would have been nice if her mom could have been here. Better than nice. To this day, Abe never pictured success without her mom in the background, a proud smile on her face. Did any child?

Today would still be a good day. A *great* day. But far from perfect.

Hope your TV has a good picture, Mom.

Abe turned her attention to the SUV's tinted window. Throngs of supporters (hecklers?) were waving flags, waving purses, waving children.

What love, what hope. Would it continue?

It's okay, Abe. It'll be fine. We've gotten through an election. Nothing is uglier than an election. We can do this.

Jim broke into her musings: "You know what to do, don't you?"

She nodded.

"You're not going to embarrass me?" he said.

"No promises."

He laughed. "As long as you don't make out with the VP again."

"Ingoing or outgoing?"

"Both."

"Too many orders, Armstrong. You don't have the authority."

"But I've got this." He put a hand under her chin and pulled her in for a kiss. A welcome one. She'd had plenty of doubts in life, personal and professional, but Jim wasn't among them.

She reciprocated, but only for a second or two. She had to keep her mind on the work at hand. The days ahead would be the greatest challenge of her life. That much was already clear.

But not as clear as it would be, only a little while later.

THE BIG CHILL...

The crowd was something to behold. An army of enthusiasm stretching nearly to the horizon, well beyond the point where Abe could make out faces.

She found herself glancing over her shoulder, reflexively searching for the source of their interest. Martin Luther King had drawn such a crowd, on this very spot. So too had the Vietnam War. But her? Abigail Armstrong?

No, it wasn't possible. They must be here for something else.

She was talented enough, but not to the point of rising above the millions. She'd always stood out in a classroom. A gymnasium, perhaps. But in a limitless expanse of bodies?

Out there, there had to be thousands more capable than her. Tens of thousands.

And somehow her preposterous plan to lead them had worked.

A senator took to the podium. The senior guy from the great state of Rhode Island. The applause was barely audible over the general din. People didn't seem to want to take their hands out of their warm pockets.

A few nice words, quickly followed by over-scripted blandness. *I joined Washington in the spirit of service; and it is in such a spirit that I appear before you today.* Abe would have liked to listen. She'd planned to relish this day. But her teeth were chattering too violently to make out very much.

January 20.

Smack dab in the middle of winter.

Why couldn't inauguration be in the spring? If she won a second term, she'd have to change that with an executive order. Forget the Constitution.

Weathermen had promised forty-five degrees at 11am, when the mics were slated to light up and the lips were scheduled to flap. Forty-five big ones. Not so bad. Skirt weather, in the northern states. Beach weather in Maine.

But the sky is a fickle thing. Some time overnight, Old Man Arctic had blown in a pocket of air that hammered the mercury into the upper teens. Now it was fifteen below freezing. Definitely not skirt weather, not even in Maine.

Abe hoped she'd applied enough lipstick to hide the blue. It wouldn't do to appear half dead. She'd be no better than the stiff that had run on the opposing ticket.

Oh well, it couldn't be helped.

January 20.

Seventeen degrees and dropping.

As the speech wore on, a stone-faced man in spectacles approached Abe: Ed Parsons, a longtime friend, soon to be her senior adviser.

She'd seen the look on his face before. His news was grave.

Abe went to get up, but Ed waved her back down.

"Everything okay?" she said.

Ed wavered. Chewed on his lips. He wasn't excited to share whatever it was that was on his mind.

"Ed, what is it?"

He sighed. "Al's going to be late."

"What do you mean, la—"

She spun around, looking for her running mate, Al Chase. The man had been in the row behind her, not two minutes back. He wasn't there now.

"He had to go back in," Ed explained.

"Everything okay?"

It was a dumb question. VPs-elect don't vacate their chairs on

Inauguration Day to have a smoke.

"Little stomach bug," Ed said. "Threw up. Which was actually a miracle, if you think of it."

"Doesn't sound like a miracle."

"He could have done it while he was taking the oath. On Lincoln's bible."

Not a bad point.

"What do we do?" Abe said.

"*You* don't do anything. Proceed as normal."

"But he goes first."

"Eh." Ed swatted his hand. "Arbitrary tradition. You go first. We'll pump him full of drugs and toss him back out."

"What do we tell the people?"

"Nothing." He squeezed her arm. "And get used to it."

The crowd swallowed every gap of space between here and the Washington Monument, a mile away. Somewhere around two million people, somewhere around half a percent of the national population.

She was going to have to face them all—alone.

"It's my show now, isn't it?" she said.

"Always has been." Ed patted her on the shoulder and retreated into the safety of the crowd.

THE SOUND OF SILENCE...

Two minutes later, the vice president's chair was still empty.

Very empty.

Little stomach bug.

Al had been a naval aviator before he'd been a congressman. Fifteen years at sea. Swells and gales and roiling seas. Those guys don't catch *little* stomach bugs.

Abe didn't allow the concern to show on her face. She needed to appear unflappable, unperturbed. This was a test of her leadership, a mild one. Though young, though her political career wasn't old enough to qualify for kindergarten, she was in charge. She could deal with a vacant chair. She could deal with anything.

The event went on. Crowds clapped. Politicians pontificated.

And then, some interminable time later, it was time to complete the business of the day. A booming voice announced her. The cheer climbed to a deafening pitch.

No sound on earth is more powerful, and more promising, than the cheers of a crowd. The chant of your name. For the first time that day, Abe felt a surge of warmth. These were her people now. Not her supporters, not her voters—her *people*.

They were with her.

Everybody was with her.

She rose, and the crowd rose with her. Enough energy to float the Mall into the air. Roaring mouths, roiling banners and sparkling flashbulbs.

All of that enthusiasm, all of that love, directed at her.

Politics has its ups and downs. More downs than ups, but nothing on earth could beat this.

Two million people, all with her.

With an almost overwhelming pang of surreality, she stepped up to the presidential podium. Her. The snot-nosed tomboy with skinned knees and pigtails. The kid who in the summertime fanned out into the nether regions of the Midwest on the jump seat of daddy's station wagon. Long afternoons on tire swings over lakes. Grills smoking away on docks. Burnt noses and peeling shoulders.

Skinny dipping one fateful evening with a boy who chickened out at the last minute, forcing her to hide her modesty with her hands…

One of which was now on the bible, the other in the air.

She was talking now, repeating words from the mouth of the imposing man in front of her. Big, booming voice. Nothing like hers. At least, nothing like the voice she heard in recordings. So nasal. So flat. Can a president sound like that?

Focus on the words, Abe. Enjoy the moment. Concentrate.

You're equal to the task.

You belong in history.

Hopefully.

Suddenly everyone went silent, even the man in front of her. In a hot, distant recess of her brain she knew that it had happened: she was the president now. No more tire swings for her. No more skinny dipping. Nothing could ever be the same, ever again.

The crowd tensed with anticipation.

They wanted her to speak.

Her?

Really?

Of course. You're here for a reason. Yes, 35% of them believe that you are the daughter of Satan. 14% believe you are Satan. 17% don't care. But the rest believe in you. Show them that you believe in yourself.

She cleared her throat, scratching those seventeen degrees out of her airways. A foolish move: this was going to be her first utterance as president. A sound, preciously close to a belch, washing down the Federal Mall like a tsunami.

Only…

It never came.

The speakers were silent.

It was okay. A technician was watching her, would only turn them on the instant she spoke.

So speak, Abe. Speak.

"Mr. Chief Justice, members of the United States Congress…"

Something wasn't right. She saw it on the faces of the crowd before she caught the sound. Lack of sound.

The Mall was quiet.

The speakers weren't working.

She turned around for help. Behind her were Supreme Court justices, former presidents, senators. People, in other words, who were incapable of fixing anything. No help would come from that quarter.

Ed…where are you?

Of course he wouldn't be there: he was probably down in the bowels of the basement, strangling the audio tech into submission.

A few murmurs of displeasure from the crowd. They too wanted to move things along. They too were eager to stop freezing.

Ed…

And then, the invasion began.

A squeal bled out of a distant speaker, rising until it sounded like a fighter jet bearing in on the crowd. In a flash it was deafening. Abe had to defend her ears with her hands, a move that would undoubtedly be memorialized in photographs. She felt a tug on her sleeve and turned to see the face of a sturdy, fresh-faced young man. Secret Service. A man who'd been trained to take her away in the event of anything unusual. Apparently he didn't know that in Washington, failure wasn't unusual.

I'm here to change that.

Please.

Move this along, Abe. Take charge.

She pressed the man's lapel, silently telling him that it was okay, silently pleading with him to get the hell out of there.

The sound died. Abe's ears settled into a dull ring. Freezing and deaf. Welcome to history, Abe. Welcome to history.

She tapped the mic. A thud bounced across the mall. The speakers were working. All was well with the world.

Time to bring this show to order.

"Ladies and gentlemen," she announced, "this inauguration is brought to you by Tylenol."

Polite laughter from the crowd. Not exactly a gut-buster, but not bad for an off-the-cuff opening, given the circumstances.

Now for the big one, the one she'd practiced every night for the past two months.

"Mr. Chief Justice," she went on, "members of the United States Congress, presidents, assembled dignitaries, and most importantly, my fellow Americans, I am humbled at the opportunity to stand before you today."

Plenty of cheers for that line. Abe gave it a moment to die down before continuing.

"Today we celebrate not the victory of one candidate over another, nor the success of an ideology at the expense of its opponent. Today we celebrate peace. We celebrate an institution that—"

The speakers had shut off again.

These damned guys. Unbelievable. One mistake was okay. Everybody gets one mistake. But two, on the same day—the VERY DAY OF HER INAUGURATION?

No more passes.

Heads were going to roll.

Executive Order Number One: polish off the guillotine.

Okay. She'd have to continue on the strength of her own voice. People had done such things before. There must have been politicians in the days before microphones.

"Today we celebrate," she began anew, "an institution that comes to us from—"

She felt a tug on her shoulder, and not a polite one.

She turned a furious eye on the compact man behind her.

Colonel Patterson?

No, that didn't work. Didn't make sense. He was a military aide, not a political one. He had no place at this inauguration. Shouldn't even be in the crowd.

His lips were moving. She shook him away and went back to the podium.

Another tug, this one nearly strong enough to throw her off balance.

Once again, the colonel's lips flapped away. She couldn't be sure, but it almost sounded like he said:

"Madam President, you need to come with me right now."

Something wasn't computing. Was this some ritual she wasn't acquainted with?

"Colonel, I'm kind of…in the middle of something."

"Yes, ma'am. You are."

FOOTSTEPS. . .

Abe's heals tap-danced across the marble of the Capitol rotunda, a hand on her elbow prodding her along.

An attack. This could only mean an attack.

Thoughts of 9/11. Bush reading a story about goats to schoolchildren.

For seven minutes, he'd been allowed to read on—to children.

Abe hadn't gotten ten seconds—during an inaugural address.

"Colonel, you going to tell me what the hell's going on?"

"Not yet, ma'am."

The colonel pushed her toward the main entrance.

"Is it terrorism? A threat to the inauguration?"

"Not yet."

She tried to spin around, but the colonel's hand kept her going. "What do you mean, not yet?" she said.

"We need to get you to a secure location."

"We're in the *Capitol.*"

"Exactly my point."

They flew out of the entrance, where the presidential motorcade awaited them.

"Where's Jim?" she said as her entourage streamed around her.

"Your husband will follow in a separate vehicle."

"Ed too?"

"He's already in the Beast."

"The Beast?"

She put her eyes on the presidential limousine, aka the Beast, aka the heaviest, most expensive four-door transport in the world. Its window were black. Impossible to tell who was in there.

"And Al?" she said. Still no sign of her VP.

The colonel shook his head. "He's ill."

As though that were an answer.

The hands pressed her on, until she was seated in the back of the limousine, the face across from hers—Ed's face—visibly older than it had been a half-hour before.

THE BELLY OF THE BEAST...

The colonel's hands did all the talking.

Articulate hands. Practiced hands.

One reached into his jacket and withdrew a key. A very small key with no grooves, only teeth. Jagged little things that bit into the metal cuff on his wrist, liberating the briefcase that was to remain bound to the colonel's wrist at all times—

That was, *almost* all times.

There was only one reason for him to unlock that briefcase.

Abe had known of the thing well before her presidency. The atomic football. The button. The case that carried the phone number for the end of the world.

The Joint Chiefs had intoned about it during her orientation meetings. How many sessions had there been? Countless. A dozen, at least. A dozen orientations wasn't much better than zero. Far too much information for any single person to retain, certainly a person with Abe's mediocre memory.

She'd reserved her gray matter for domestic concerns. The public and the laws it lived by. Seemed like important stuff at the time.

She'd spent a little time with lifers from the State Department, memorizing the names of foreign presidents and prime ministers and the troubles they faced. But it was too much. Just memorizing the layout of the federal government was beyond her abilities, bureaus upon agencies upon departments. Fiefdoms as far as the eye could see.

Not much room to memorize launch codes in there. Fleet movements and troop positions and strategic responses. That had been her VP's responsibility. Al had never shied away from the ugly stuff.

But Abe remembered the football.

"We have confirmation of an ICBM launch against the United States," Patterson said.

The landscape beyond the windows was a blur. The Beast was really moving.

The sun had poked out from behind the clouds. Maybe the temperature would move up a little. Might even crack twenty degrees.

Twenty degrees isn't so bad. Better than seventeen. Shouting distance from the freezing point. The people on the Mall would be pleased with the change. Not so bad for a January in Washington.

"Madam President, did you hear me? We have an attack in progress."

No, she wasn't sure she'd heard him. His words didn't make sense.

Abe shook her head. "What are you talking about?"

"We detected the launch three minutes ago." He withdrew a headset from the football, hit a button, didn't like the result. His face wrinkled with confusion.

"You guys move fast," Abe said.

"Not fast enough. We've got—" the colonel glanced at his watch "—a little more than thirty-two minutes until probable impact."

Abe was supposed to ask questions, now. Lots of questions that relied on a great deal of foreknowledge. Generals to call and men to mobilize.

But she found herself unable to voice them. She pictured flashes in the sky. Shockwaves. Cities turned to dust under a sky that wouldn't see the sun for months. Years.

Unless she figured this out.

"We have a lot of decisions to make," the colonel said.

32 MINUTES TO GO. . .

In a flash, Abe realized that they'd made a mistake.

A glaring, horrible, obvious mistake.

But one that could be easily repaired.

"Stop the car," Abe said.

Nothing happened to the blur behind the windows.

"Did you hear me? Stop the car."

"Abe," Ed said. "What are you trying to do?"

The driver didn't even acknowledge that he heard her. Abe banged on the glass partition behind his head. She might as well have been smacking the glass on Shamu's tank. Inches upon inches of Plexiglas. Built to resist large-caliber bullets and, it would seem, off-script instructions from the president of the United States.

Her armrest was a mess of buttons. She'd never had time for a primer on the limousine. The controls for the window must be down there somewhere. She hit a switch and a vent blew frigid air into her face.

"Jesus," she said.

I don't even understand the Executive Office well enough to open a window.

"Abe, slow down," Ed said. "What's the problem?"

"Miller," Abe said.

That being former President Miller—former, as of about ten minutes ago. Traditionally, no great friend of Abe. They disagreed on nearly everything. But something told her that neither of them wanted to fry in a nuclear holocaust.

"What about him?" Ed said.

"We need to pick him up."

"He isn't the president anymore."

"He has experience."

"Nobody has experience with this," the colonel said.

The latter hit a button on his headset and didn't like what he saw. "The Joint Chiefs have already moved to code red—DEFCON 2. They don't want to go beyond that without your authorization."

Abe kept the frozen vent on her face. "Where's the missile going?"

"We need to get with the Pentagon," the colonel said. "Damn satellite phone isn't connecting." He dropped the headset and fumbled with the buttons on the armrest. "Any idea how to work this thing?" he said to Ed.

Ed leaned forward and studied the armrest. Fidgeted with a few, got Abe's vent to climb a few degrees.

"Jesus Christ," Ed said. He sat back and smacked the window until somebody up there saw something. The window came down, revealing two men. A driver and passenger. Neither of them turned around.

"They cleared?" Ed said to the colonel.

"They're Secret Service," the colonel said. "They're all cleared."

Ed turned to the driver. "You know how to operate this thing? The phone?"

The man next to the driver responded: "I don't have access to the com link, but I can patch you through to whoever you need."

"I need the National Military Command Center. The Pentagon can connect you."

The man up front placed a call, spoke through several directories in private, then forwarded the call to the cabin's speakerphone. The world erupted with the sound of ringing.

First triumph of the day.

"Sheridan," the phone answered.

General Dwight Sheridan, Chairman of the Joint Chiefs of

Staff, the most senior officer in the US Military. Aside from the scripted briefings, Abe had met him twice. Once had been a handshake, the other a two-minute policy discussion on the funding of overseas bases. Her brief impression had found him to be humbler and more self-effacing than she'd expect in a general. More George Clooney than George Patton.

The colonel began the call: "General Sheridan, this is Scott Patterson. I have the president in the car."

Sheridan said, "Madam President, we are just over thirty minutes from probable impact."

Thirty minutes. A sitcom with all the commercials. A simple recipe. A flight of an ICBM.

"How many missiles?" Abe said.

"At the moment, our detection network is only picking up one. Obviously a good sign. This doesn't look like the start of a broader campaign."

"Do you know where it's going to land?" she said.

"Preliminary tracking suggests it will strike the East Coast of the United States. Given that most ICBMs carry multiple warheads, it's possible that it will target several cities."

"Was it North Korea?"

She could deal with North Korea. Her advisers had primed her on the possibility. An isolated launch from limited power. Not a good start to her presidency, not by a long shot. But at least it wasn't a prelude to global nuclear war.

"No," the general said, "the Russians."

Abe took some time to process that response. The Russians had done it. Good news and bad. The good: Russia had no reason to want a war against the United States. The bad: there was no way to win a nuclear war against Russia.

Abe said, "I need to speak with President Yakushev immediately."

"We're efforting that, ma'am."

"But don't we have that special phone, that red phone—what's it called?"

Abe's eyes were on Ed, but it was the general who responded.

"Not anymore, ma'am. These days we only have a priority email address. Nobody's responding."

"Try his regular phone."

"Nobody's picking up. Same story for all of our backchannels. My people are speeding through the Rolodex."

"Get somebody on the phone, General. This has to be a mistake. We've got to get the Russians to hit the self-destruct button."

"Russian ICBMs don't have that capability."

This bomb had just gotten a lot uglier.

"How is that possible?" she said.

"We don't have it either. Our war scenarios proved that self-destruct capabilities increase the chance of nuclear conflict."

Abe wasn't in the mood to explore that point. She closed her eyes.

"How many people will it kill?" she said.

"If the warheads land—*if* they land—they will be lethal for more than five miles in all directions."

Five miles in all directions. How much area would that cover? Abe recalled the equations of grade school: to get the area of a circle, multiply the radius by itself and then multiply the result by three. The answer was seventy-five.

Seventy-five square miles carved out of the East Coast's biggest cities.

"What do we do?" Abe said.

Sheridan allowed the question to hang in the air for an uncomfortable span. At long length he responded:

"That, Madam President, is up to you to decide."

The motorcade sped on.

30 MINUTES TO GO. . .

The car lurched to a stop, and the door opened into chaos.

A battlefield of roaring helicopters, bellowing fire engines, blaring police cars, platoons of men in every uniform conceivable.

It took Abe a few seconds to realize that she was standing on the White House South Lawn. Ordinarily a scene of well-manicured serenity. Not today.

The colonel came up behind her, his voice a shout above the din. "We've already instructed the Warrenton operations site to expect you. It's our best option, given the timeline."

His hand ushered her toward a helicopter.

"You mean we're leaving?" Abe said.

"They'll have full communications ready for us when we arrive."

"How long will it take to get there?"

"The site's in northern Virginia. We can have you there in twenty minutes."

They kept trotting toward the helicopter.

"How long do we have?" Abe said. "Before the bomb lands?"

"We'll cover that in the bird."

"You said it was a little over thirty minutes?"

The colonel glanced at his watch. "Actually, now it's a little *under* thirty minutes. We have to get moving."

Abe fought his hand, slid to a stop.

"We're going to spend most of that time in the chopper," she said.

"It's fully linked, ma'am. You'll be able to coordinate our response in the air."

The helicopter was a hundred feet away. From here, it was loud enough to rattle the roots of Abe's hair.

"You expect me to make my decisions in *that thing*?" she said.

"We don't have a choice. Warrenton's the closest command shelter outside the anticipated blast range."

"What about the bunker downstairs?"

The colonel shook his head. "We don't go down there, not if we have forewarning. We can't afford to get stuck in Washington."

"My *job's* in Washington."

"I understand that, ma'am. But right now we need to be concerned about getting you to safety."

"What about the city? Isn't that my concern?"

"Ma'am, with respect, we really don't have the time."

"That's my point, Colonel. You want me to gobble up our time in that thing. I won't be able to think. I can't make my decisions in there."

"The bunker isn't secure, not against a direct impact."

"Colonel, I'm not leaving. Take me down there."

After a long moment of hesitation, the colonel stepped away and conferred with one of the Secret Service agents.

She read his lips: "The president wants to go to the PEOC."

The agent looked at her. His mouth and his eyes said two very different things. The mouth nodded, but the eyes said that she wasn't ready to make these kinds of calls.

29 MINUTES TO GO. . .

For the first time since stepping onto the lawn, Abe caught sight of Jim, coming out of an SUV. Over the protest of her security detail, she ran over and wrapped her arms around him.

"Are you still the president?" was the first thing he said.

Apparently he put great stock in inaugurations.

Abe almost laughed. Nodded. "Did they tell you what's going on?"

"Some kind of international emergency," he said.

"The Russians launched an ICBM."

Jim's face blanked out. "Where?"

"Everywhere."

More hands on Abe's elbows. That seemed to be the order of the day. The agents barely trusted her to walk, and they expected her to fix this nightmare?

A crowd pulled her and Jim across the lawn.

"Jim, listen," Abe said as they approached the West Wing. "I need you to call my mom—"

Abe turned around, saw the colonel battling the crowd. "Where's the safest place for people to go?"

"This kind of strike," he said, "it doesn't matter."

They passed between a pair of implacable Marine sentries. The Marines always guarded the West Wing. Always. Night and day, rain and shine. What would they do during a strike? Stand out here and watch?

As her entourage entered the building, Abe turned back to Jim.

"Tell her to keep away from the window."

So pathetic, so inadequate.

But her mother was way out there, in the remotest corner of flyover country. As safe as any spot could be.

Back to the matter at hand…

"Where's the secretary of defense?" she said to the colonel.

They were nearing an ancient elevator, doors open. As he drew up the colonel stood aside and gestured for Abe to enter.

"The acting secretary will meet you downstairs," he said.

A handful of agents joined them in the elevator. The doors snapped shut and the motor shuddered into action.

"I want Pratt," Abe said. "Not the acting—"

"Your appointee hasn't been confirmed yet. If you decide to…" The colonel paused, measured his words "…If you decide to *respond*, you'll need confirmation from the acting secretary."

A man Abe had met all of one time.

She exhaled with a long string of ugly words.

28 MINUTES TO GO. . .

The doors opened into an ancient, cramped corridor. Stale air tinged with peroxide; the smell of a doctor's office, way back when. Hushed voices. Stark fluorescent bulbs. Agents doing their best to look as if Abe's entrance were a matter of routine.

The agents shuffled Abe and her husband across the terrazzo tiles, toward a t-intersection.

"I'll take you to your office, sir," one of the agents said to Jim.

Apparently Jim was going in the opposite direction.

Time to part.

A quick glance, plenty of tension in both sets of eyes. There was nothing to say, and no time to say it anyway. Jim grabbed the back of her head and kissed her. A quick one, and sullied by the probing eyes of agents. But not bad. Jim always had it where it counted.

Off he went, down the other corridor.

Abe approached the command center with tentative steps. This was to be her first performance as president. The room wasn't much, as such places went. A long table of two-dozen chairs, only half full. Four carafes of coffee, three plates of pastries, mostly donuts. Somebody had actually thought to bring donuts down here.

Aside from the agents, only one face in the room was familiar: Acting Defense Secretary Donaldson. A thick head of snow-white hair. A holdover from the prior administration.

Not a single member of her NSC was present. Her National Security Council. The people who'd been hired to help her through such crises.

The chairs were crowded by monitors on the walls. Lots of heads floating up there, none of them talking. The show hadn't yet begun.

She was the show.

Okay, Abe. This is it. You took the job for days like these. Well, maybe not exclusively for days like these. Magazine covers aren't too bad. Stadiums full of adoring supporters aren't too bad either. But the job is about work, and today is certainly going to be work.

You can do it. Hold up your head and plant a grim, authoritative line on your lips.

One, two…

Everybody stood as she entered. Even the people on screen. What a strange new world, this was going to be.

Abe nodded them into their seats and scanned the screens. She recognized a few of the faces, most notably General Sheridan. One display showed a host of statistics Abe didn't understand. Another showed a cable news broadcast, teargas and rioting in Moscow.

The last showed a sketch of the world as viewed from above the North Pole, green continents superimposed on black oceans. A thin red line toward the top, beginning in southern Siberia and ending a third of the way to the North Pole.

The line grew a few pixels as she stared.

"The vehicle is passing over the Central Siberian Plateau," said Acting Secretary Donaldson.

Prior to today, she'd only shaken his hand a single time. What would she have to decide with this man? Who would die on their watch?

"When can we stop it?" Abe said.

"If you'll take your seat." Donaldson looked at the chair at the middle of the table.

"We can stop this," she said. "Can't we?"

He looked pleadingly at that chair, as if it could somehow bail him out of an answer.

As it turned out, another voice did the job:

"Madam President, if I might begin…"

The voice was General Sheridan's. A handsome, square-jawed GI with just a little more pepper than salt in his hair.

Abe took her seat. "Please do," she said.

He drew a breath and went on with remarkable speed, setting the tempo for all the discussions that followed. Voices overlapping. No time to pause. No time to think.

"Lots of parties are listening in on the day's proceedings," Sheridan said, "but in the interest of brevity, I'll only point out a few. We have all the Joint Chiefs, as well as the commanders of US European Command and US Northern Command. We have Ambassador Rains to the Russian Federation, together with CIA Moscow Station Chief Martinez. Unfortunately, the president's NSC is en route to the Warrenton operations site. A hiccup in communications, I'm afraid."

"Can they be conferenced in?" Abe said.

The general cleared his throat. "Their bird doesn't have that capability. Nothing secure."

Meaning no NSC, not until it was too late.

Meaning Abe was all alone.

Sheridan went on. "We're waiting for Vice President Belman, who's en route to his residence. I know he belongs to the prior administration, but his replacement hasn't yet been inaugurated. Technically, Belman is still the vice president."

The general paused. He must have caught Abe's glare.

She should have realized this: her VP hadn't put his hand on the bible, so his predecessor was still in office. Belman wasn't an ally, not in any sense of the term. A popular journal had written that Abe was a big middle finger to the previous administration. Not a particularly nice description for any parties involved.

But Belman would bring experience. Much needed experience. Abe should be grateful.

Sheridan went on. "We have a side line, which will be briefed on some of the items we'll be discussing. On that line are the British prime minister and NATO's secretary general, among many others. I'm going to ask people with questions or concerns to enter them into the queue; otherwise please leave the talking to me and the people in the West Wing."

The people on screen nodded, but no one said a word.

"Madam President," Sheridan said, "do we have your authorization to elevate our forces to DEFCON 1?"

"General," Abe said, "you need to tell me if we can stop this."

"Ma'am, we're on it. But if you will, we have a number of priority decisions that need to be made immediately."

"When?"

"Right now, ma'am."

"No, I mean the missile. When can we shoot it down?"

"We're setting up an intercept in the Arctic Ocean. Launches in a little over ten minutes."

"Will it work?"

It was a simple enough question. Anybody would expect the president to ask such a question. Undoubtedly the general had prepared a measured response.

And what was this response?

The man looked away from the camera. Broke electronic eye contact.

Such was the government's confidence in its countermeasures.

Abe primed him again. "General?"

"We hope so," he said. "We all hope so."

27+ MINUTES TO GO. . .

Sheridan went back to his earlier inquiry. "Ma'am, do we have authorization to go to DEFCON 1?"

DEFCON 1—the highest state of defense readiness. Signal of imminent nuclear war. Of imminent *defeat*, more or less.

It had never been seen before, not even during the Cuban Missile Crisis, when Kennedy was all but certain of annihilation. Abe was being asked to order it ten minutes into her presidency.

"How will the Russians take it?" she said.

"They've launched a missile against us. They're expecting it."

"Very well, General. You have my authorization."

"COGCON 0 as well?"

Abe was less familiar with the concept—from what she recalled, it handed the country over to armed federal agencies, allowed them to seize and confiscate and destroy whatever they wished. Allowed them to hit the so-called internet kill switch. Take control so the mob couldn't.

"Do you recommend it?" she said.

"This is a crisis. We need maximum flexibility to deal with it."

Not exactly a straight answer.

"I'm not in the mood to turn off our democracy," Abe said. "Not without proof it's necessary."

Sheridan studied her for a beat. "You'll have it soon enough."

The words hung in the air as he conferred with someone out of frame. Then he turned back to the camera. "May we at least go to COGCON 1?"

Much less invasive.

So she remembered.

Once upon a time, Abe had refused to make a decision without reams of analysis. The content of her speeches, length of her TV ads, color of her banners. Now she was transforming the country on the basis of vague recollections.

She nodded. "Yes, you may go to COGCON 1."

Sheridan passed on some instructions, then continued. "Here's what we know. At 12:14 EST, NORAD's Satellite Early Warning system picked up an infrared signature in the area of Drovyanaya, southern Siberia. Subsequent analysis has confirmed that the signature is that of a UR-100N intercontinental ballistic missile. Given the probable flight path, detonation will take place roughly thirty-five minutes after launch, though the time will vary depending on the eventual target. We anticipate a payload of three warheads, each yielding one megaton. While it's possible all three will descend on a single city, it's likely they'll split up. That's how most Russian missiles are programed. Therefore we believe the major cities of the Northeast Corridor are at risk: Boston, New York, and Washington."

Sheridan's voice picked up a little hesitancy. "In the event of successful detonations, we expect US fatalities to stand between five and ten million."

26 MINUTES TO GO. . .

We expect US fatalities to stand between five and ten million…

Abe looked at the donuts as she heard the words.

She wasn't sure she could ever again eat a donut.

She put her eyes on Sheridan. "How is the public reacting to the news?"

Sheridan said, "Ma'am?"

"The public, General. I want to know how they're dealing with this."

"They are, ah, presently unaware of the situation."

"You mean you haven't told them?"

Sheridan took the answer as self-evident.

"General," Abe said, "they're about to get bombarded with three million tons of TNT. You don't think they have the right to know?"

"Preserving order is of the utmost importance."

"Saving *lives* is of the utmost importance—"

"It's the same thing, Madam President. We have two million in and around the National Mall. If we tell them, they'll panic, stampede. People—*many* people—will die."

"How many more will die if we don't tell them?"

"There's no place for them to go, ma'am."

"People who are outside during a nuclear blast—what happens to them?" Abe said.

"They're dead either way," the general said.

A new voice chimed in: "That's not true."

It was Ed Parsons, her chief adviser. Somewhere during the proceedings he'd slipped into the room.

"I have some research here," he said. He fixed his glasses as he thumbed through a report. "In this kind of impact, most of the fatalities would be caused by burns. People are much safer indoors, where they're protected from the heat of the blast."

"And you want them to fry outside," Abe said to the general.

"I don't want to cause a panic," Sheridan said. "Rule number one in a crisis: only share actionable information. We don't have shelter for all these people. There's nothing they can do with the news."

"Put them in the museums on the Mall," Abe said.

"*Two million people?* Ma'am, with respect, they'll panic immediately. Crush themselves to death. Threaten a total breakdown of law and order—in a place we very much need to control. We've played games on these scenarios before. They always end badly if we notify the crowd."

Abe leaned back, chewed on her lip, looked at the kindly face, the professorial face of Ed Parsons.

"They want me to leave two million people on a field," she said, "in a nuclear attack."

Ed didn't look pleased at the prospect.

Abe went on. "After evacuating that very field myself. Everybody'll think I saved myself and left the rest to fry."

"Your two million closest supporters," Ed said. "You could very well face impeachment. Or worse."

"I can't leave them out there, Ed."

"No, Abe, I don't think you can."

"Madam President," Sheridan broke in. "We must move on to other issues."

Abe looked at the man. "General, I want you to send out an emergency broadcast."

"With respect, ma'am, that's a mistake."

"Then it's my mistake. Send out the warning."

The general blinked at her. Made it clear he didn't like the way this went.

Then he passed along the order.

25+ MINUTES TO GO...

"We need to formulate our response."

Sheridan's tone made it clear that he was shifting to more substantive measures.

Abe welcomed the shift. Not that it would be easy. They had countermeasures to go through. Missile defense screens, the probabilities of success, the anticipation of waiting to learn the results.

But at least it would take her mind off the people on the Mall. The two million souls who somehow, somewhere needed to find shelter in the next twenty-some minutes.

"You said you're going to attempt the interception from the Arctic," Abe said. "What backups do we have in place?"

"Ma'am," Sheridan said, "this isn't the time to talk about missile defense."

Abe shook her head. "Is there some other defense I don't know about?"

Lasers. Reagan had been obsessed with lasers.

But not obsessed enough, Abe was quickly learning.

"I'm talking about neutralizing the enemy's capabilities," Sheridan said. "It's the only way we can ensure the public safety."

Neutralizing capabilities. Abe was no veteran, but like anybody who'd ever tuned in to CNN, she was well aware of the military's obsession with sterilizing the obscene.

He was talking about nuclear retaliation.

Killing millions to save millions.

In theory.

25 MINUTES TO GO. . .

Sheridan went on: "Before we get to that, we have to understand what's going on with the Russians."

He shuffled papers off camera and went on, speaking so fast that Abe had trouble following. "We've been studying and simulating nuclear war for seventy years. A big part of this is signals intelligence—what our enemy's moves indicate about their intentions. They have not mobilized their armed forces. They've launched a single missile, a land-based one at that. That's a crucial point. The Russians have ballistic missile submarines, capable of striking coastal cities within three minutes of launch. If they wanted to take us out, they'd send a barrage of nuclear warheads from our coasts on depressed trajectories, decapitating our command and control. Then they'd—"

"General," Ed broke in. "Where are you going with this?"

The general paused and reshuffled his thoughts. "A single ICBM from a distant location is a gift in comparison. We can see it coming, have time to respond. The Kremlin is smart enough to realize that. Do you think they'd risk a disastrous counterattack just to get out a single pot shot?"

Abe said, "Ten million fatalities is a pot shot?"

The general winced. "In military terms. Strictly military. This is the work of a rogue. Protocol dictates that a single launch from an isolated site is the work of a group operating in contravention of Russia's Strategic Rocket Forces." The general looked down, to scan his notes. "Two additional facts support this. First, the launch site is the most remote in Russia from any significant concentration of troops, making it the easiest—for lack of a better term—to seize. Second, Russia is on the verge of civil war, one that has caught us by surprise. For what it's worth, the Russian ambassador in Washington believes the launch must be the work of a rogue actor. But he's not in contact with Moscow."

Abe turned her eyes to the image of Ambassador Rains, of the Moscow embassy. *Acting* Ambassador. Like most of the people in today's meeting, she was a relic of the previous administration, soon to be replaced. Nothing personal, just executive business.

"Ambassador," Abe said, "can you offer a little flavor?"

The ambassador stirred. "Only what I can see out my window, which is more than I'd like." She cracked a tense smile. "Our liaisons were ejected from the Kremlin this morning, before the launch. But there are riots all over the city. Red Square is a mob scene."

Red Square, a place Abe had seen only in movies. She pictured Clint Eastwood sporting a fake mustache, sneaking down cobblestone streets. Tom Hanks complaining about toothaches as he ran packages across an endless expanse of brick.

Presidents were supposed to have time to come up to speed on such things.

"The picture outside is grim," the ambassador went on. "The police have closed off the roads surrounding the embassy, but crowds are massing at our walls, throwing bottles over the gates. It would appear that Admiral Sharapov's supporters dislike the US almost as much as they do President Yakushev."

Don't get the names wrong, Abe. Whatever you do, don't get the names wrong. This woman has lived in Russia the better part of her adult life. And she's looking to you for guidance.

Abe said, "Is it possible that…Sharapov is behind the launch?"

"Unlikely," General Sheridan butted in. "Sharapov is with the navy. Rocket guys don't get along with the navy guys. Rockets think they're superior."

"Madam Ambassador, do you agree?" Abe said.

"He's always talking about rebuilding Russia," the ambassador said. "A nuclear war is a pretty bad way to do that."

"This is a good thing," Sheridan said. "Sharapov has wide-reaching influence. Hopefully the rogue actor does not."

Abe's blood pressure lost a few millimeters of mercury. This didn't mean all-out nuclear war. This was a single missile, fired by a rogue actor. She could handle this.

Only five or ten million fatalities...

"So it's clear," Abe said to Sheridan. "This is an isolated attack. No need to strike them back. We have to focus on shooting this thing down. How do we stand on that front?"

Sheridan hesitated. "I've told you about the one, in the Arctic. We have another option as well. But I must tell you that our track record is mixed, at best. ICBMs fly four miles a second. It's extremely hard to hit a small target moving so fast."

"Where's the backup system?" she said.

"We'll get there when the time comes. But interceptors are step two."

"Step two? What's more important than saving ten million people?"

"Saving the rest."

MEANWHILE. . .

The music stopped.

That's when things began to turn.

It was strange, how abruptly the president had vacated the podium. Unprecedented, one of the news anchors had said. And ominous.

But the people in the Mall—they knew better.

The instant President Armstrong had stepped away, a man had taken the microphone and explained everything.

"There's been an international incident," he said. "One that requires the president's immediate attention. She's been keeping a close look at the situation and insisted on receiving all news immediately. There's no cause for concern, at all. The president will be returning shortly to complete the inauguration."

She was coming back.

No cause for concern.

No cause at all.

The sound technicians filled the air with music. Patriotic marches, from the baton of John Philip Sousa. Rousing stuff.

Enough to replace Honest Abe? No, perhaps not. But plenty, to give the place a feeling of excitement. Of *adventure*.

An inauguration interrupted, because of an international crisis.

An audience with a first-hand view of history. Who got that kind of thrill anymore?

People began to dance. It wasn't exactly club music, but they made it work. There was a lot of laughter in that audience, a lot of enthusiasm. Honest Abe didn't care about pomp and circumstance. If work needed to be done, she got it done, damn the consequences.

If only all of Washington worked that way.

That's why they'd elected her.

Why the better part of them loved her.

The fourth song was a repeat, which was strange. Almost as if the people on the podium had stopped paying attention to the day's proceedings.

A glitch, someone in the audience explained. Exactly what had happened when Abe's mic didn't work.

The festivity went nowhere. If anything, people became even more excited. It was so different, this inauguration. So fresh.

So when the music cut off, the people were thrown into confusion. Why end something that was working so well?

The crowd went silent; and for the first time since it had convened, conversation became possible.

Russia, somebody said. It must be Russia.

A revolution.

A new Cold War.

Maybe it would be best to leave, a few of the attendees said. Before the rest of the crowd gums up the whole city.

But no, Abe would be back. Nobody wanted to miss that.

After some moments, the music came back on, and for a few seconds the festivity continued. But then that too was interrupted, only this time silence wasn't the culprit.

Instead, it was a rasping sound from all the phones in the crowd.

The older people among them recognized the sound: a dial-up modem, trying to connect. The sound of the early internet.

Then the speakers came alive once more.

Only it wasn't music this time. It was a voice, somewhere between man and machine. On phones the voice was accompanied by block letters:

EMERGENCY ALERT SYSTEM

EAN NETWORK ISSUED AN EMERGENCY ACTION NOTIFICATION

—THIS IS NOT A TEST—

A NUCLEAR ATTACK IS OCCURRING AGAINST THE UNITED STATES.

ALL RESIDENTS OF THE UNITED STATES ARE ADVISED TO SEEK OUT AND PREPARE TO TAKE SHELTER IMMEDIATELY. IF YOU KNOW OF A NEARBY LOCATION THAT HAS BEEN DESIGNATED AS A FALLOUT SHELTER, GO THERE NOW. OTHERWISE, GO TO A BASEMENT OR OTHER INTERIOR ROOM ON THE LOWEST FLOOR OF A BUILDING. DO NOT USE ELEVATORS. LOCK ALL WINDOWS AND PLACE AS MANY OBJECTS BETWEEN YOURSELF AND THE OUTSIDE AS POSSIBLE.

HAVE A BATTERY-POWERED RADIO FOR YOUR STAY IN THE SHELTER, TUNED TO STATIONS PROVIDING NEWS AND INFORMATION FOR YOUR AREA. THE PRESIDENT WILL BE SPEAKING ON ALL STATIONS SHORTLY.

THIS IS NOT A TEST.

FURTHER ALERTS TO FOLLOW.

Some of the cannier attendees told their compatriots that this was no cause for worry. History had brought many false alarms. There was no reason to think this was any different.

Except the president had vacated the podium, with nary a word of explanation from her mouth.

Sounded a great deal like a threat from the sky.

A threat to Washington—one that was very likely aimed at the ground beneath their feet.

The stampede began before the voice finished its first loop…

23 MINUTES TO GO...

What could be more important than saving ten million people?

Saving the rest...

This was how the general had responded to Abe's question.

These were the people who were now at risk.

Not ten million.

The rest.

Abe spoke to Sheridan's disembodied head. "I don't understand."

Sheridan didn't look like he was in the mood to explain.

Abe tried again. "General, are you suggesting that we should retaliate after a *rogue launch*?"

"Strategic protocol, Madam President. In the event of an unauthorized launch, protocol dictates that we must consider the entire launch facility compromised."

"And what do we do with a compromised facility?" Abe said.

"We neutralize it."

Neutralize. There was that term again.

"Which means exactly what?" Abe said.

"We deploy our own nuclear resources against the facility."

"You want to repay the compliment," Abe said. "Fight nukes with nukes."

The general didn't respond to that.

"You think the Russians will sit back and watch the missiles fly?" Abe said.

"As I've explained, we believe this was the work of a rogue

actor. The Russians will expect it."

"I don't know how you can say that. We haven't heard anything from the Russians."

"The Drovyanaya launch site is home to twenty-one known missile silos, each housing a UR 100-N ICBM. I'll remind you that this is the result of covert intelligence; American representatives have never been admitted to the site. Each missile is capable of carrying up to six warheads. We believe that most are carrying three. With one missile launched and twenty remaining, a total of sixty warheads remain at the site. Enough to destroy sixty large metropolitan areas. We've run scenarios based on this set-up; I'll ask my people to put them on screen."

The wall screen with statistics went blank and then flashed a list of cities:

CITY (PROBABILITY OF STRIKE)
CHICAGO, IL (93%)
LONDON, UK (92%)
LOS ANGELES, CA (90%)
HONOLULU, HI (88%)
HOUSTON, TX (86%)
FAYETTEVILLE, NC (82%)

…

All of America's major cities and domestic bases, and many of its allies'.

If the protocols were correct.

And if the generals were telling the truth.

22 MINUTES TO GO. . .

Which was an important point.

So far, Abe had heard of nothing but chaos coming out of Russia. Certainly nothing coordinated enough to land bombs on Washington.

"General," she said, "How can you be sure it isn't an accidental launch?"

"I'm sorry?"

"A mistake. An unintentional twist of the launch key."

"Our analysis suggests that's all but impossible."

Abe asked him to elaborate.

"First," General Sheridan went on, "we have the general upheaval of the country. Suggests the possibility of a coup against their nuclear forces. Second, the Russians aren't taking our calls. That's suspicious. If it were an accident, they'd be scrambling to tell us about it. Better to be embarrassed than dead. But if somebody seized control of a facility—that's a different story."

The general collected his thoughts before continuing.

"In that case, they'd do one of three things. First, they could remain silent, which I believe they're doing. Second, they could lie, tell us it's an accident. But that could soon be proved wrong, with follow-up launches. Then we wouldn't trust them, would suspect some grand scheme—would commit to a comprehensive counterattack. Third, they could tell the truth. Russians never do that, because they think we wouldn't believe them. They think that we'll expand on their claim—interpret an admission that one site is compromised as an admission that ten are compromised. Or more."

"If one facility is compromised," Abe said, "what makes you think that more aren't on the way?"

The general didn't have an answer for that question.

MEANWHILE...

Once more, dinosaurs fell victim to an intruder from the skies.

Recognizing the hopelessness of traffic, the complete jamming of the subway stations, the crowd rushed toward the big museums lining the Federal Mall.

For the first several seconds, the thousands of police in attendance were able to keep the crowds at bay.

For the first few seconds.

But as the crowds pressed from behind, as the people in the fore lost the ability to direct traffic on behalf of the whole, the barriers fell back, the police with them.

By the time the crowds reached the doors, the press of bodies was already too great to allow the former to swing open. People found themselves shoved against the glass, their smothered chests unable to draw breath.

And then the glass burst, and the crowd poured in. No employees kept count of admissions. No fire marshal warned about excess attendance.

The bodies piled in.

The warning hadn't specified the time to impact. It could be minutes, the people surmised. Seconds. People will do anything, when their children are seconds away from annihilation.

Many more doors and windows followed the fate of the first. Within a minute of the initial damage, the Natural History Museum already looked as if it had suffered a great calamity.

Rather inconvenient, for a place that was to shield against a nuclear attack. But in the frenzy of escape, nobody noticed this. The crowd was rushing, so everyone should rush.

Somewhere inside of the second minute, the first artifact fell victim to the feet of the inrushing stampede: a stegosaurus skeleton awaiting refurbishment in the basement; then followed a meat-eating allosaurus who'd spent the past few decades menacing the stegosaurus.

The shards infected the worst of the crowd with a lust for pillage. Soon many more displays followed suit, artifacts that had survived centuries of weathering succumbing instantly to the frenzied fingers of the mob.

People who only minutes before had convened to celebrate the peaceful ascendance of a hopeful new candidate.

The spirit of destruction washed up the stairs of the museum and across the lobby. It grew purer in the crush of humanity. The crowd grew so thick that those in the halls could no longer descend the stairs. They piled into every last nook they could find. Display cases. Guard booths. Toilet stalls.

Two million people, crowding into a few thousand square feet.

A NUCLEAR ATTACK IS OCCURRING AGAINST THE UNITED STATES.

Amidst the shouts and shatters, the first victims fell. Almost no one attempted to help them up. The logic of panic had taken grip. In a stampede, it's safer to step onto an outreached hand then to take it in yours.

21 MINUTES TO GO...

Back in the bunker, far quieter but equally tense, Abe spoke:

"I can't believe this," she said.

The looks on the other faces suggested everybody was in more or less the same boat.

She elaborated. "In eighty years, the Russians never lost a silo. Not to the Mujahideen, not to the Chechens—not to the angry masses, when the Soviet Union collapsed. Now you're telling me they gave the keys to a madman?"

"They didn't give anything, ma'am," General Sheridan answered. "They were taken by surprise."

"How? I've got this guy carrying a suitcase full of numbers because you need codes to launch. No codes, no launch. You telling me the Russians skipped that step?"

The general answered by looking at somebody else.

"General," Abe went on, "a single actor can't launch the missiles. We have safeguards."

No response.

"Is there something you want to tell me?" Abe said.

No response. Whatever, or whoever, was sitting to the General's right was more interesting than the president.

"Something you *don't* want to tell me?" Abe said.

Finally, the general responded. "I'm going to turn this over to General Quinn, commander of Air Force Materiel Command."

His camera panned over, revealing a somber, pale woman. The latter offered a generic greeting, which Abe returned.

General Quinn said, "I can't speak directly for the Russian program. But there *are* ways for a single individual to arm and launch one of our nuclear weapons."

"Meaning that a single person can kill ten million?" Abe said.

Quinn didn't answer that.

Abe pressed on. "Is this the result of an oversight or plan?"

"Both, ma'am."

"You're telling me that this—" Abe nudged the nuclear football, which the colonel had set on the table in front of her "—is bullshit?"

"Abe," Ed said. "We need to keep moving."

"I am moving, Ed."

"Not bull—" the general shifted in her seat. "We have a two-man rule in place—for everything. From the order to launch—issued by you, confirmed by the Secretary of Defense—to the turning of the keys at the launch consoles. Every step requires two people."

Abe massaged her temples. She wished they'd left a tray of aspirin on the table.

"Forgive me, General. Time is short. Can a single man arm and launch one of our nuclear missiles?"

General Quinn hesitated. "Yes. But they're never allowed back into a silo once they take possession of that information."

"What if they break into a silo?"

The general didn't respond.

Another general not responding.

Abe leaned back and looked across the table at Ed. "We're in deep shit," she said.

20 MINUTES TO GO...

"The warhead has entered the Arctic Circle."

This time, General Sheridan had broken the silence.

Abe looked at the map. The red line had stretched, oozing down the screen like a drop of blood.

Soon enough, missile defense would have its chance.

It was time to put the subject of *response* to bed.

"What exactly are you proposing to do to the Russians?" Abe said.

"I'm not proposing anything," Sheridan responded. "I'm reciting protocols laid out by people smarter than me."

People who weren't in this room. People who like unseen Gods had hammered their rules onto a tablet and expected their descendants to follow them without question.

"Fine," Abe said. "So those people want me to fire a nuke, take out the compromised facility? Is that the idea?"

For the first time that day, Sheridan looked uneasy. He cleared his throat. "I'm afraid the Russians have planned for this contingency."

"Meaning exactly what?"

"Their silos are too far apart to hit with a single warhead. Protocol requires two warheads per silo, to ensure adequate damage. Forty warheads in all."

Ed was beginning to look claustrophobic.

"We can't use a conventional weapon?" he said. "A bunker buster?"

"Not against a Russian ICBM silo. They're not nearly powerful enough."

"What would the total yield be?" Ed said.

"About twenty megatons," Sheridan said.

Twenty megatons. The equivalent of forty billion pounds of TNT, in a single strike.

"That's more firepower than we dropped in all of World War Two," Ed said.

Sheridan had a guilty expression as he responded. "I believe it's roughly…four times as much."

MEANWHILE. . .

The war suffered its first fatality.

Ella Brennerman of Philadelphia, an elderly woman whose grandmother had campaigned for universal woman's suffrage.

Ella fancied the idea of a woman president, but she fancied Abe Armstrong even more. A lady who ran for president without ever trying to exploit her gender. Or betray it. Abe was a woman who could stand with the men without trying to become one. A feminist, of a form that would have made Ella's grandmother proud.

These thoughts were far from Ella's mind in the last seconds of her life. She had disregarded the warnings of her fellow celebrants; she was too old and too alone to run for cover.

Terrorists were attacking, they said, and aliens and asteroids and viruses too.

Maybe all the stories were right. Ella didn't care. She'd rather die in peace than live in a frenzy.

But the crowd didn't let her.

Someone tugged her along; she thanked him but insisted she was fine. He left. Another tug, another thank you, another departure. But the third tug was different. More insistent. Thinking it was a policeman, she turned to thank him away. But it wasn't a cop. It was a nice-looking young man, in the sense that he must attract young women. He didn't look kind.

He tugged again, the strap of her purse snapping against her neck.

Now Ella understood.

"Okay," she said. "You can have it."

She tried to help the man get it off. He seemed to think she was resisting. Pushed her to the ground and tore off her purse.

Thirty dollars, keys to a Buick and row home on a depressed block, a pill case full of generics, and an ancient compact. These were the things that had sent Ella to the ground.

She was okay. A little shaken up, but nothing that a long soak in a tub wouldn't remedy. She took a moment to catch her breath, planted a foot on the ground, prepared to stand. At that moment something slammed into her, flipping her onto her back. In her daze she expected a voice—*Are you alright?*—and a helping hand.

Neither came.

But a boot did.

After the first trample she still believed she would get up. But the second and third told her different. Soon enough she knew the stampede would never stop, not in her lifetime at least.

20- MINUTES TO GO. . .

Things in the bunker moved even more quickly.

Words overlapping words, people speaking and listening at the same time. Listening, but not really thinking. There wasn't time.

But Abe needed time. Back in World War Two, the allies had six years to drop five megatons' worth of bombs. Now the generals were asking Abe to quadruple that in a few minutes.

How could she do it?

How could she know it was the right way to go?

Abe ran her hands through her hair. "What proof do you have?"

"Ma'am?" Sheridan said.

She stood. "You're asking me to believe that the Russians—some of them—have launched a nuclear missile at us. How do I know that's true?"

"It's been confirmed by our warning system."

"These warnings have gone out before. False warnings." Abe snapped her fingers. "Ed, you know what I'm talking about. The Russians thought we were launching against them."

"Stanislav Petrov," Ed said. "That's the Russian who picked up a bogus launch from the US, way back when."

"That was a different time and a different detection regime," the general said.

"Did he pick up a launch?" Abe said.

"He detected an anomaly."

"And what did he do?"

"He guessed that it was a false alarm. Correctly."

"*Correctly*, general."

The general didn't look pleased with the course of the conversation. "That's a bullshit story. Forgive my impertinence. That guy picked up a single blip on a single monitor. Even the Russians required multiple-source confirmation. Their protocols would easily have identified the warning as false."

"So why the story?" Abe said. "Russians like to fess up to their meaningless mistakes?"

"Takes the focus away from their meaningful ones."

"Madam President," said the snow-haired Secretary Donaldson. Until now he'd been mostly silent, sitting quietly at a chair halfway down the table. Taking it all in. Judging the new administration.

He went on. "The Petrov story is irrelevant. This is a different situation. Totally different." He looked up at the map. "We've tracked the vehicle with satellites and radar stations."

"But no human eyes," Abe said.

"We have a dozen separate confirmations of this launch," Donaldson said. "It's real."

"Maybe it's not a mistake," Abe said. "Maybe it's an illusion. A computer virus. A demon holding visions of apocalypse before our eyes."

"We have an air wall," Donaldson said. "There's no connection between our defense networks and the internet."

Ed couldn't hold out any longer. "Did the Iranians have an air wall?"

"The Iranians don't have nuclear weapons," Donaldson said. "Not last I checked."

"Only because we hit them with a virus," Ed said. "A network that was supposed to be insulated from the outside world."

Abe was familiar with the topic—a virus written by American and Israeli operatives had crippled Iran's nuclear enrichment equipment.

"The Iranian network picked up the virus via a flash drive," Sheridan responded. "We're smart enough to prohibit any such devices on our detection networks."

"But you allow radar signatures," Ed said.

Colonel Patterson cut in: "We now have less than twenty minutes until impact."

Ed leaned in. "General, you know that a hacker doesn't need a traditional entry point to infect a network. Computers can be hacked with high-frequency sounds. Who's to say our detection array can't be hacked with radar signals?"

Abe turned her eyes to Sheridan. "Are we chasing ghosts?"

The general didn't respond, but this time he didn't seem to be evading the question. He was thinking. Actually thinking. He'd never considered this question.

Until then Abe hadn't considered that the general was barely more prepared for this conversation than she was.

MEANWHILE...

The man saw that his position was hopeless.

In the blind panic that had followed the announcement he'd followed the crowd. The Natural History Museum was a safe bet, the people seemed to think. An old building. Thick walls. As close to a shelter as they were going to find on short notice.

But the secret was out. The building looked like a picnic basket on an anthill. Little creatures swarming everywhere.

Somehow, for some reason, many of the windows were blown out.

A bomb?

He couldn't press on anymore. Too many people. He found himself doing terrible things. Shoving women out of the way. Children. Clawing at faces to stay on his feet.

It couldn't continue this way.

He had to come up with a better option.

The roar was deafening. He saw men throwing fists and kicking legs; he saw men and women being trampled to death, their bodies tossed about like sacks of grain.

He checked his phone, rescanned the message from the Emergency Alert System. So vague. A NUCLEAR ATTACK IS OCCURRING AGAINST THE UNITED STATES.

What kind of attack? National, regional, local? Was it concentrated on Washington—on the inauguration crowd?

It could be anything, from a dirty bomb in the subway to the hijacking of a nuclear power plant. The man had no idea how much time he had.

If it was a dirty bomb, he might not hear anything. Might feel nothing as the invisible radiation tore apart the atoms of his body...

This was all wrong. He couldn't be here. A crowd was the worst place to be in a terrorist attack.

He had to level his head. Clear his thoughts. Figure out a better way.

Trampling feet, all around him. Tumbling bodies. Screaming mouths.

These people weren't the way. To follow them was to die.

He turned around and jumped. Got a view over the crowd. Gobs of people in all directions—except for a patch, off toward the Capitol. The crowd seemed to be avoiding that building. Perhaps it was intimidated by the enormous barriers erected to protect the inaugural podium.

But those barriers were largely unmanned. Certainly less dangerous than the press of the crowd.

And in all events, it was better to be shot on a wall than radiated to death.

He set off for the Capitol. He didn't notice that he'd caught the attention of a number of others, all desperate to follow somebody with a better plan.

19 MINUTES TO GO . . .

"Madam President," General Sheridan said, "if I may, the clock is ticking."

Abe was aware of that. The map screen had a countdown clock, numbers big enough to swallow all of Asia.

"If the rogue is readying additional ICBMs," Sheridan went on, "the window to preempt them is shrinking. It takes only twenty-five minutes to prep their missiles for launch. We have to assume they're doing it as we speak."

"That's exactly my problem," Abe said. "All assumptions, no facts."

"No different from life," Secretary Donaldson said.

"We may have to assume some things," Sheridan said, "but we're not assuming a launch. It's been validated."

"So you say," Abe said. "We've seen it only through the eyes of a network. They can be hacked."

Sheridan said, "For a third party to hack into our networks and create the illusion of a launch—tracking from dozens of different detectors—is inconceivable."

"More inconceivable than a guy seizing control of a silo that's hundreds of feet underground?" Abe said. "A silo guarded by the most elite troops in the Russian military? And now that we're on the subject, how do we know the rogue isn't operating remotely? That he didn't hack the Russian launch computers? Maybe he has access to their whole arsenal."

"Extremely unlikely," Sheridan said, "as any defense expert in the room can attest."

Defense expert. Emphasis on *expert*. A word that swept up everyone in the room but the one-term senator from Michigan.

A vacated term at that.

18 MINUTES TO GO. . .

But it really wasn't eighteen minutes. The uniforms were pressuring her to make a launch decision—now.

With almost no information. Just a few lines on a screen.

Russian ICBMs. Nuclear retaliation. Silos and launch codes and thin red lines.

It was unreal—ancient history, cold war stuff. Things best left to former actors with supernaturally black hair. The US didn't have much of an anti-nuke movement anymore, because most people assumed they were on the way out.

They are on the way out—of the silos.

"Madam President," Sheridan said. "Have you reached a decision?"

The room's eyes turned to her. Her eyes turned to other things.

Buildings blown apart. People running around—deaf, burnt to the bone and bleeding from the ears. Injured children screaming for parents who'd never answer.

This was the price of a bad decision.

The general was right. If she failed to act, the rogue could seize the rest of the launch facility. Could send sixty more megatons in her direction, spelling the end of America. And quite likely, the end of civilization.

But what was the alternative? Forty warheads in the other direction. Forty blips on the Russians' radar screens. If that wouldn't look like the beginning of an all-out nuclear war, nothing would.

Burnt faces.

Screaming kids.

Millions of them.

"Madam President—"

She slammed her hands, sending a wave of flinches around the table. "I heard you the fourth time, General."

A few seconds of silence followed. A rare break in that room.

Secretary Donaldson broke it. "I know what you're going through."

"Do you?"

His voice grew sharper. "We have families, same as you. Loved ones who are going to die in twenty minutes. The question is, how can we save the rest?"

"You tell me, Mr. Secretary."

"We eliminate the Russians' ability to launch additional weapons."

"You want to launch forty nukes? In response to one?"

Donaldson nodded. "It's the only way to end this thing, once and for all."

MEANWHILE. . .

They approached in a thin gray line. Countless numbers of people.

The Capitol police officer considered his orders as he watched them:

Hold the line…under no circumstances is the public to be permitted to enter the Capitol…

The faces of the people coming this way—pure desperation. Nowhere to go. They might as well try to fight a tidal wave.

How was he going to hold them back?

Something told him the barriers wouldn't do the job on their own. Three layers of Plexiglas between him and a sizable chunk of the two million who'd attended today's celebration.

A good number of the faces were bloody. Broken noses. Bleeding lips.

Not celebrating anymore.

He screamed at them with a megaphone. Crowd control model. Loud enough to be heard over any racket, the ad had said.

Not loud enough today.

The crowd pressed on.

The desperate faces grew nearer.

Behind the officer, in the congressional bunker, nearly three quarters of the nation's legislators were taking shelter. If the building fell, the government would fall with it.

"Stay back!" he shouted into his megaphone. "Do not cross the barrier!"

A teargas canister flew into the crowd, smoking like a red-hot charcoal. It struck a man in the head, sent him down like a sack in a chute.

He disappeared under the stampede.

Another canister.

The crowd kept coming.

A pulsing roar from the steps to his side: another officer had turned on the LRAD—a sonic weapon that repelled crowds by bombarding them with noise powerful enough to churn stomachs and burst eardrums.

A few people fell over. They too disappeared under the feet of their peers.

The crowd kept coming.

The officer shouted again. The frontrunners were twenty yards from the first barrier. Desperation had become fury. They didn't look like they were fleeing, they looked like they were attacking.

It was time.

Well past time.

The officer drew his pistol, fired it into the air.

No response from the crowd.

They kept coming.

The government was relying on him. His *country* was relying on him. The needs of the many, and all of that. He had to do it.

He put the gun on the crowd.

Where to aim? There were so many of them, out there. Any choice would be arbitrary.

It wouldn't be a child. In no case would he shoot a child.

Or a woman.

A pale face stood out from the others. Alabaster-white, from the cold. A man, just on the cusp of middle age. A ringleader, perhaps.

He would have to do.

The officer lowered his gun to the center of mass, put his finger on the trigger. He had to shoot. His duty required it.

But what would it accomplish? If the people couldn't hear the megaphone, they wouldn't hear his shot.

And they wouldn't see the results, not through all those bodies.

It would be nothing more than murder.

An innocent, running for his life.

How was an officer any different from the runners? Once they crossed the boundaries, the officer would be among them.

He had to run.

Now.

And there was only one place to go. He fled up the steps of the Capitol, entered the rotunda, kept going as the surge of bodies enveloped him.

Someone had battered down a door. The bunker was open.

Like water, crowds fleeing calamity flow to the lowest point.

They poured down the steps.

17+ MINUTES TO GO . . .

"General," Abe said, "even if I assume our trackers are correct, I—"

A wave of the general's hand cut her off. He conferred off camera, grabbed a telephone, talked in a hushed voice.

Something unexpected had happened.

Another launch?

Abe looked at the map, half expecting another thin red line, or perhaps only a new dot that hadn't had time to grow a second dimension. But nothing of the kind had happened. The original was still alone, but much bigger. Much closer.

"Okay," Sheridan said, returning to the camera. "I don't know if anyone's noticed, but our Moscow embassy has dropped out of the call. We haven't been able to contact them. We're awaiting an explanation."

"Theories?" Abe said.

"Our embassies have satellite phones and generators, can contact us no matter what's happening to power and communications in their host cities. If they've gone silent, it has nothing to do with the equipment."

"The ambassador said they're under attack," Abe said. "You think they've been overrun?"

Sheridan shook his head. "We would have gotten a distress signal. I think they're preoccupied. If the facility's in imminent danger, staff are ordered to wipe their drives and burn their documents. If I had to guess, that's what they're up to."

"Where do they go when they're done?" Abe said.

"The Marines will determine whether evacuation is viable."

"And if the Marines don't think it is?"

"Trust me," Sheridan said. "They'll think it's viable."

"Tehran all over again," Ed Parsons said.

"We'll keep the group advised," Sheridan said. "We need to get back to our response."

Tehran all over again…

Decades with no direct communication between nations…

"General," Abe said. "If I give you an instruction, can you relay it to them?"

"I'll send a secure SMS to their satellite phone."

"Please order the embassy staff to remain in place."

The general shifted in his seat. "Ma'am, it's as your own adviser said. It could be another Tehran. An entire embassy taken hostage. We can't afford that."

"You're asking me to sever our most viable link with the Russians. I can't do that. I need to hear something before I make my decisions."

"I'm afraid war doesn't work that way, ma'am."

War.

That was the first time anybody had risked the term.

"We need to change our thinking," Sheridan went on. "The Russians very well may remain silent until all of this is over. We have to be prepared to respond without a conversation."

MEANWHILE. . .

Down in the Capitol bunker, a senator heard a curious noise.

A rumble, behind the bunker's thick metal door. An explosion?

Not according to the reports. Just a little disturbance out on the mall. Nothing to trouble the people in the bunker.

Bunker—hardly. Perhaps it had passed for a bunker in 1870. A basketball court hallowed out of the dirt beside the Capitol Crypt.

Not even enough chairs for all the people in here. Nobody had considered families when designing this place. The junior members were forced to stand.

This place had independent ventilation and blast-proof doors, according to the Capitol Police. But they never said anything about the roof. Overhead and a little to the side was fourteen million pounds of cast iron—and that was just the dome. Who knew how much more the building weighed? At least as much. Twenty-eight million pounds just begging to bury Congress.

The noises kept coming.

A little disturbance out on the Mall.

The senator looked at a neighboring colleague. The latter shrugged. Didn't seem concerned. But something was odd. Not the noises themselves; they sounded like nothing so much as slamming doors. But the fact that the senator could hear anything through three inches of steel—that was strange indeed.

An auditory illusion, probably. The sounds of the ventilator echoing across the chamber.

Only...the ventilator had gone silent. Who would turn off the air conditioning of a crowded bunker?

The door boomed. Shuddered. Groaned.

Was it opening? The police said it would remain shut until the crisis was over.

Maybe that was the answer: they were safe. The threat had been nothing more than a false alarm. A fly on a radar dish.

But then the door burst open, crushing a guard against the wall, and a flood poured in. That's what it looked like. A liquid mass of people, far too many to count.

The congressman fled with his friends and adversaries to the back of the space. But he couldn't go far. There wasn't enough room, nor enough air. Not even close.

The crowd pressed on.

16+ MINUTES TO GO. . .

"We are prepared for our first defensive countermeasure."

General Sheridan's voice carried a new tone. Optimism?

A fair enough reaction. If the countermeasure worked, this meeting could disburse. Success against one ICBM would point to success against others. No more need to discuss responses. They could keep their forty warheads stowed away while the state department figured out how to coerce Russia into repaying its mistake with a century of supporting votes on the UN Security Council.

All eyes were on the map. A dotted red line beginning in Siberia and ending on top of the world.

The placement confused Ed Parsons: "Ah, general, the nuke is still over the Arctic Ocean."

"That's correct."

"Last I checked, we didn't have a GMD site at Santa's Workshop."

"But we do have a Virginia-class submarine that's outfitted with our upgraded Aegis Combat System. We were able to break through a thin spot in the ice."

"Aegis missiles can't hit ICBMs," Ed said.

"This one can."

16 MINUTES TO GO...

"Madam President," Sheridan announced, "it has been over twenty-five minutes since launch."

"Thank you, General."

"May I remind you it takes that amount of time to launch a Russian ICBM."

That might be true, but it didn't mean all that much. If the rogue had control of the facility, he could have initiated new launches at any time.

New launches at any time...

"General," Abe said, "are you surprised that they haven't launched more missiles?"

"I was surprised enough they launched one."

"You're missing the point. If the rogue had all the missiles, he'd have launched them by now. He hasn't launched. He doesn't have control."

"Madam President," Secretary Donaldson said. "You're the one who's missing the point."

That point, among many others.

"Go on," Abe said.

"The rogue doesn't have control of the facility," he said. "That's why we have a chance to nip this thing in the bud. We can neuter the son of a bitch—if we launch *now*, in accordance with protocol."

"Who came up with your protocols?" Abe said.

"Millions of war simulations."

"Who designed the simulations?"

"Committees, Madam President. Teams of experts."

There was that word again. *Experts*. It always came across as an epithet, in this room.

"Did they predict this?" Abe said

"If you can think it," Secretary Donaldson said, "we've run it."

"So what happens if we do what you're recommending?"

"Ask me what happens if we don't."

"First answer my question."

"Just over fifteen minutes to impact," Colonel Patterson butted in. "We have confirmation of the weapon's targeting. Northeast corridor of the US, as anticipated."

Donaldson's eyes had remained on Abe. "Your question begs a prejudicial answer," he said.

"Sounds like you don't like the answer," Abe said.

"I don't," Donaldson said.

"And yet you expect me to go along."

"It's a matter of probability," Donaldson said. "If we execute the protocol, the statistics say that we can expect half of the US population to die in the ensuing conflict."

Abe shook her head. "This is the course of action you *want* me to take?"

The secretary nodded.

"I'm having…trouble seeing the payoff," Abe said.

"The statistics look a lot worse if we don't."

MEANWHILE...

Word spread quickly across the Mall.

Rumor had it that thousands had been admitted into the bunker of the Capitol. Plenty of space down there, a manmade cave secured by a thousand feet of bedrock.

But there was a problem with the news.

For the people on the west end of the Mall, the Capitol was impossibly remote, on the other side of a mob whose ranks had scarcely thinned into the museums.

But to the north was an equally large expanse, one that was almost entirely empty.

"The White House has a brand new bunker," a man said. "Able to take a direct hit from a nuke. I saw it on the news."

"They were fools to go for the Capitol," said another. "The White House gets all the security."

"I hear they got space for the whole city."

They turned north.

15 MINUTES TO GO. . .

"We should talk about Dead Hand," Sheridan said. "That'll help the president understand the stakes."

"This conversation is pointless," Donaldson said. "We know what protocol says—"

"Sir," General Sheridan said, "The president has the right to know. Everyone in the room has the right to know."

Donaldson waved a hand. "Take it away."

Sheridan said, "Dead Hand is a way for the Russian corpse to punch back."

Abe held up a hand, cutting him off. She'd heard of this before, not from a briefing, but a drunk admiral at a campaign party.

The Dead Hand program was designed to ensure that Russia could retaliate after a nuclear attack. No matter the state of Russia's command and control, upon the detection of a nuclear strike—seismic activity, light and heat emissions, radiation emissions—the program would automatically execute a massive retaliation. Hundreds of warheads launched from a graveyard. Enough to kill everyone in the US, even if there wasn't a single Russian alive to see it.

"I know about Dead Hand," Abe said. "Hardly makes me want to launch, General."

"Which is why you have to know about it," the general said.

Abe's mind had twisted into a Gordian knot. Protocol was telling her to launch; the general was telling her that protocol might get them killed.

The logic of nukes.

More than ever, it was clear they had to stop this thing.

A yellow line was tracking up the map, toward the North Pole. The Aegis interceptor.

"General," Secretary Donaldson was saying, "you know Dead Hand is disabled."

"Sir, I don't know that."

"If a rogue seized control of their site," Donaldson said, "the Russians would be insane to initiate the protocol."

"If they think we'll respond with a massive strike, they'd be insane not to."

"We're not striking anyone," Donaldson said. "Half our boomers are parked off our own coast."

Donaldson rubbed his face, turned to Sheridan's image. "I think you should be a little more straightforward."

"Sir?" Sheridan said.

"You said it yourself," Donaldson said. "She has a right to know about everything. *Everything.*"

A lot of emphasis on that last word.

The two men stared each other down electronically.

14+ MINUTES TO GO. . .

Sheridan took a call, listened, hung up after a few seconds.

"Word from the embassy?" Abe said.

Sheridan shook his head. "We're getting reports of casualties on the Mall."

"The Mall? You mean the Federal Mall?"

"Apparently the announcement sparked a panic."

Her announcement.

Abe swallowed, closed her eyes. "How many?"

"We've lost contact with the authorities. We're not even getting through to the Capitol."

"What's happening up there?"

"Reports are unreliable in the first stage of a crisis, Madam President."

Interesting words, from the general. Abe allowed them to float in the air. *Reports are unreliable in the first stage of a crisis.* If that was true for millions of people under the wide open sky, it had to be true for missiles screaming across the sky at nearly twenty thousand miles per hour.

But Abe didn't dwell on it. She had a new problem.

She said, "Are you suggesting that people may have broken into the Capitol?"

"They know a nuclear attack is underway. They'll run into bullets to avoid the bomb."

"Is this happening anywhere else?"

"My sources indicate the answer is, *yes.*"

"Yes, as in scattered places?"
"As in everywhere."

MEANWHILE...

The fastest runners are the first to die...

The words ran on a loop in Lance Corporal Rodriguez's mind as he stared over the barrel of his M240 machine gun.

INSTANT JUSTICE, read the stencil on his stock. It had seemed appropriate enough when he'd put it there. It didn't feel so appropriate now.

The terrain in front of him was clear. A great big circle of grass, directly to the south of the White House. The bullseye for an incoming nuke, the Marines used to joke. Had that joke ever been funny?

Hard to believe, a crowd of thousands was drawing near the trees on the other side of the park. Soon enough he'd see them. The last report put the front line on Constitution Avenue, a thousand feet from his position.

The man beside him went by *Brick*. Short for Brickman. He was watching a monitor. "Jesus, they've taken the Capitol," he said.

Rodriguez caught sight of movement in the trees. But it was wind, only wind. No runners yet.

The fastest...first to die...

Like the Capitol Police, he'd been trained for circumstances like these. But unlike the Capitol Police, Rodriguez was a Marine, a branch that responded directly to the orders of the president. The president had ordered DEFCON 1. Imminent nuclear war. So the Marines were at war.

First to fight.

Rodriguez tested his grip and swung the gun, staring at the

trees through his sight. Any second now. An inauguration crowd, US citizens, people fleeing the bombs that some psycho had fired at them.

Rodriguez felt a tingle on his scalp. A guardhouse was no kind of place to ride out a nuclear war. Plywood walls and asphalt shingles, piled onto Pennsylvania Avenue in the rush after 9/11. A temporary structure that had somehow managed to become permanent.

He caught a blink to his right, and swung his sights.

A man was breaking through the trees.

"Twelve o'clock," Brick said.

"I've got him," Rodriguez said.

A voice boomed overhead. "THIS IS THE MARINE CORPS. DO NOT APPROACH THE WHITE HOUSE FENCE. DO NOT APPROACH THE FENCE OR YOU WILL BE SHOT."

Womp—womp—womp. The acoustical weapons were going off.

Rodriguez still had the guy in his sights. Moving fast. A hell of a runner. He was winning the day's first prize. Lucky him.

Rodriguez flicked the safety.

"Come on," he said as he stared the man down. "Be smart, you bastard. Stop. For both of us."

The man kept running.

Then Rodriguez saw that he wasn't a man. Fresh face. Lanky build. Long hair. It was a kid. A fucking kid. Probably a track star.

"Brick," Rodriguez said to the man beside him, "tell this kid to hit the deck."

"I would if I could," Brick said sadly.

The kid was closer now, almost across the circle of grass, a bunch of swift-footed friends behind him. He was coming directly for the guardhouse.

The LRADs blared on. *Womp—womp—womp.*

The kid looked goofy. Like a class clown. Like the guy who got pizza delivered during math finals.

Probably showed up today because his parents had wanted him see a little history first hand.

Too first hand. Way too first hand.

A voice over the radio: "Give him a warning shot, Rodriguez. Make sure he hears it."

Mary, full of grace.

Rodriguez raised the barrel and swung it a little to the right. It was a clean shot. He'd been trained to fire warning shots directly to the south. Right into the Potomac. No harm, no foul. If his aim was true.

He slipped his finger. Took a breath and squeezed.

Rap—rap—rap.

The kid dropped as though he'd taken a bullet. He stayed there a second, then kneeled and patted his stomach. No wounds. He took to his feet.

And he kept coming.

In a few seconds he'd closed all but the last thirty yards.

"Do not let them touch the wall," said the voice in Rodriguez's earpiece.

"What do you expect me to do?" Rodriguez said into his mic. "Splash a fucking kid?"

"Do not let them touch that wall," came the reply.

Rodriguez's body numbed. Fingers, feet and brain. Gunny couldn't be serious.

The kid was a dozen yards away. Rodriguez put a bead on his chest. He'd never fired at living tissue before. Not even an animal.

His finger felt the warm metal of the trigger. The sharp knurling of the grip.

The fastest runners are the first to die.

"RODRIGUEZ, WHAT ARE YOU WAITING FOR? TAKE THE SHOT."

It was over. Had been over, since the minute he came out of boot camp.

Never disobey a Gunnery Sergeant.

Rodriguez pulled the trigger. The barrel coughed. The boy hit the ground.

The first of many.

14 MINUTES TO GO. . .

"I want to talk about Dead Hand," Abe said. "I can't do anything until I understand how the Russians will react."

"We don't need to worry about Dead Hand," Donaldson said.

"With respect, sir," Sheridan said, "I disagree."

"Only because you're ignoring the most important part."

That being the part Sheridan refused to talk about.

"General," Abe said, "you don't want to be the one who withholds information from the president during a nuclear crisis. Life will get ugly for you. I promise you that much."

Sheridan mulled that over and said, "The Russians have the Black Book."

Abe's eyes passed to the nuclear football, idling on the table in front of her. *The Russians have the Black Book.* She understood the words, but not their collective meaning. The statement made no sense.

Secretary Donaldson rephrased it more starkly: "The Russians know our strike protocols. Most of them."

"You mean they stole them," Abe said.

"We handed them over. Willingly."

Scattered coughs around the room. The sounds of chairs squeaking. Feet passing by the door.

What was this place? Who were these people? We gave them thousands of nukes, an arsenal built with trillions of dollars, defended with secrets so inviolable they aren't even entrusted to presidents-elect of the United States, only to have them spill their guts to the enemy—
THE VERY PEOPLE OUR ARSENAL WAS DESIGNED TO

PROTECT US AGAINST?

Calm down, Abe. There's a reason for this. Ask for it. Process it. Make *decisions* on the basis of it.

She cleared her throat. "Forgive me, I'm no defense *expert*. Why in the hell would you share that—" She pointed at the nuclear briefcase. "—with them?" She pointed at the top of the map.

"Some of it," was all the general said.

Abe worked her fingers into her forehead. "Allow me to understand. You guys classify everything. The inseam of a general is classified. And now you're telling me it's all bullshit? We reveal our souls to people who launch at us without provocation?"

Secretary Donaldson cut in. "Only to help them interpret our moves. They know we're going to respond against the compromised site—and only the compromised site."

"That we *may* respond," Abe said.

Donaldson smiled with frustration, shook his head. "The Russians know that we'll limit our strike to the compromised site. For that reason, they won't enable Dead Hand."

"If a rogue initiated the launch," Abe said, "how can we even be sure the Russians know about it?"

Donald's smile became a grimace. "Please."

"We haven't heard a peep from them," Abe said. "Not a word of apology. Don't you think they might drop us a line, if they knew they'd just started World War Three? And it's as the general said: they haven't mobilize their forces. Doesn't sound like a country that's launched a nuke. Who's to say they're not being jammed? Maybe they're totally blind."

"In which case they won't know about our counterstrike," Donaldson said. "So we're in the clear."

"Unless their communications come back while our missiles are in the air," Abe said. "Their screens could light up to show a few dozen missiles flying their way, courtesy of the US—during a coup. How do you think they'll interpret that? Maybe they'll think I'm sending over an inauguration gift."

"The Russians know about the launch," Donaldson said.

"We don't know that. We don't know anything. And you want to launch?"

Abe needed to see a friendly face. She put her eyes on Ed, who responded with an encouraging nod. *Go on, kid.*

But she couldn't. Suddenly she had nothing more to say. Her mind was as blank as the map on the wall. A sea of black, a few faint outlines, and a thin red line, stretching ever deeper into the void.

13 MINUTES TO GO. . .

An extra pair of Secret Service agents planted themselves at the door.

Almost as if they feared for Abe's safety.

She looked at Sheridan's image. "What's going on topside?"

"The White House detail is…engaged in a firefight."

Abe scoffed. "The Russians land a team of guerillas?"

Sheridan shook his head. "The inauguration crowd."

"What do you mean the—don't you check the crowd for guns?"

"I'm not involved in domestic security. But no, I don't think the crowd has guns."

"Then how are they in a gun fi—"

Then it hit her.

It wasn't a gunfight.

Oh my God.

Abe said, "You're gunning them down."

"Ma'am," Sheridan said, "we have no choice but to—"

"You didn't think you should tell me about this?"

"We have three megatons descending on the Northeast Corridor. We have an entire nuclear command structure awaiting our instructions. We have a rapidly shrinking response window. We don't have time to talk about this."

"WE CAN'T GUN DOWN AMERICANS."

"Ma'am, if you want to retain control of the White House, I assure you: we don't have a choice."

They'd already failed.

Even if they knocked the nuke out of the sky—Americans had gunned down Americans. On the White House lawn, of all places.

On the first day of her presidency.

And the bad stuff hadn't even begun yet. Not if the generals were correct.

Sheridan went on. "We cannot allow the White House to be compromised."

"We're underground," Abe said.

"You made the decision to send out the EAN," the general said. "Against my advice."

"What could I do, General? The people watched me vacate the podium. They deserve to know why."

"Do they have a right to stampede?" the general said. "To be crushed to death? To be fired upon by my men?"

Bodies riddled with bullets, littering the White House lawn.

A lawn Abe had run across, only a few minutes back.

It couldn't go on like this. Under any circumstances. Not on her watch.

"General," she said, "please tell your men to stand down."

Sheridan looked like he wanted to reach through the screen and slap her in the face.

"General," Abe said, "did you hear me?"

"Ma'am," the general said, "I'd be violating my duty if I let you come to harm."

"Please tell them to stand down."

"I'd be violating my duty if I hung my men out to dry."

"We need to get back to the task at hand."

"We won't *be able* to get back to the tas—" The general paused, reconsidered his approach. Spoke a few words off camera. Directed Abe's attention to another screen on the wall.

A new image, taken from on high, probably the roof of the art gallery a little to the west of the South Lawn. Beautiful day out there. Sunshine pouring down, despite the cold. Lawns as green as summertime.

And they were littered with bodies, most clustered at the base of the White House fence. Their ranks were growing. Somehow, for some reason, the crowd kept pushing forward. Every second, more bodies dropped. And yet they kept coming.

Why didn't they stop? Why couldn't they see it was futile?

Because they see what you see. Flesh on fire. They'd rather plunge to death than burn. Exactly as they did on 9/11.

"If we drop the perimeter," the general said, "we will lose control of the White House."

"Are any of the victims children?" Abe said.

"I have men in there," Sheridan said. "*You're* in there. So are your people. We won't stop the killing if we silence the guns. But the mob will be in control, not you. Is that what you want?"

"DOES THAT LOOK LIKE CONTROL?" Abe threw an arm toward the screen. The bodies were forming piles. Like some kind of pattern.

Abe waved over one of the Secret Service agents. "Coordinate with the Marines. I want an orderly evacuation of all personnel still above ground. Bring them into the bunker."

"No," Sheridan said. "We're going to shut the blast doors."

"General, the doors stay open. We're going to pull back our men and shut down those guns."

"That won't accomplish anything," Sheridan said. "The crowd knows about the bunker. Everybody knows. They'll find a way to break in. Or do you plan to let them in too?"

Abe kept talking to the agent. "Open up the garage, get a few men to guide the crowd in. It has to be better than nothing."

The agent nodded his way out the door. The general seemed to have lost interest in the argument.

Abe looked at the map and saw why.

"Intercept missile is nearing the target," Sheridan announced.

I2 MINUTES TO GO. . .

It looked like a video game, like that ancient arcade favorite where you try to shoot down incoming missiles.

Two lines, one red, the other yellow, slowly converging on each other. A box now appeared beside each—latitudes and longitudes, altitudes, speed and headings. It looked simple and pure. Like a math problem.

An ICBM leaves Drovyanaya at 12:14pm and heads north, accelerating to eighteen thousand miles per hour. An Aegis interceptor leaves the vicinity of Santa's workshop at 12:32pm, and also heads north (the logic of trans-polar trajectories), accelerating to nearly the same speed.

What time will they meet?

The lines were only a few pixels apart. Not a movement in the room. Not even a blink. Anticipation filled the space like sawdust, thickening the air, eating its sounds.

Abe did her best to squeeze the lines together. The same way a person might telepathically lift the home team's baseball over a fence. But no matter how hard she strained, she had no impact. The lines were on tracks that had been set by the universe itself. Movements preordained by Newton and Heisenberg, motions of planets and subatomic particles, some predictable by man, some not.

A few pixels more.

They didn't have time to watch; they had enormous decisions to make. *She* had enormous decisions to make. But she was paralyzed. Couldn't move herself any more than she could move the lines. Even her chest was still. She wasn't breathing. Had her heart required an iota of conscious attention she would have gone into cardiac arrest. The lines were everything.

A few pixels more.

Screams broke through the silence. A child, wailing.

In Abe's imagination the map had morphed into an image of a girl. Maybe a girl. It was hard to tell. The face was a rough charcoal mask, its only hole the mouth that was screaming, oddly pink and smooth and soft against the rough mess of the skin.

Third degree burns up to seven miles away. A fourteen-mile diameter. 154 square miles. A circle more than twice the size of Washington.

A few pixels more...

MEANWHILE...

Rodriguez knew he wouldn't make it, but at this point he didn't care.

He threw his weapon aside with disgust, its barrel red hot from overuse. He didn't know how many people he'd killed. Dozens, at least, starting with the boy. Jeans and sneakers. The class clown.

"We have to pull back," Brick said. "POTUS's orders."

Rodriguez motioned for his buddy to go first. They'd never trained for retreat. Not on White House duty. They'd trained to stand their ground, even against an overwhelming force.

Rodriguez would stay true to his training.

"I'll cover you," he said to Brick.

Brick paused in the doorway, gave a confused look. "With what? You're almost black on ammo."

Rodriguez pushed him through the tunnel door and slammed it shut. Brushed his uniform, straightened his cap, and stepped into the open air, air that in minutes would burn in an alphabet of radiation—alpha, beta, gamma rays.

He held out his hands and shouted. Already the first free man was on top of the fence.

"SIR—PLEASE STOP," he said. "WE HAVE A DESIGNATED ESCAPE SITE."

More people came over the fence. They weren't listening.

"WE HAVE A FORTIFIED GARAGE. ENOUGH ROOM FOR EVERYONE."

It wasn't true. Not by a long shot. But for any of them to survive, the panic had to end.

The crowd kept coming. Rodriguez stood directly in its path. He could turn around and run; he'd almost certainly be able to escape into the tunnel.

But he couldn't. Not after what he'd done.

The first man passed by, then the fence collapsed in the momentous surge. In a moment the crowd was on Rodriguez, a tsunami of people.

Only at the last minute, as the wild faces closed in, did Rodriguez think to pray.

But by then it was too late.

12- MINUTES TO GO. . .

"One hundred miles," said Colonel Patterson. "Twelve seconds."

All faces toward the map. Not a stir in the room. Not even a breath.

Abe closed her eyes. Saw the missile tearing across the lower reaches of outer space. A place that would cause our fate, but never feel it.

Flashes…blasts…screams…

"Two seconds."

Pain in her hands. Fingernails digging into palms. Strains on every muscle in her body. Soon enough she was going to have to breathe again.

"One."

Please God.

She braced herself for good words. *Direct hit. Successful intercept. Thank God.*

They never came.

ii+ MINUTES TO GO...

Silence choked the room.

Abe ratcheted open her eyes, not certain that this was a safe place anymore. The rest of the room did the same. Colonel Patterson lowered the screen of his laptop. Set his eyes on the table and kept them there.

Nobody wanted to speak.

The lines on the map were touching, according to the pixels. The resolution wasn't fine enough to show the separation. In almost every way possible, those two bombs had met. A few feet apart after a journey of thousands of miles. An extraordinary feat of engineering that had accomplished all of nothing.

More silence. Lots more silence.

Finally Secretary Donaldson cleared his throat. "As I was..." Hoarse voice. No strength. He loosened his collar. "As I was saying, there are risks associated with departing from protocol."

A child's face, screaming, everything burnt away but the pale, pink tongue...

"Which are?" was all Abe managed to say.

Slowly, the room came out of hibernation. Chairs shuddering forward, mouths coughing, hands rubbing faces.

"If we depart from protocol," Donaldson said, "the Russians won't know what we're doing."

"The Russians must prefer no missiles," Abe said. "Protocol or not."

"That's not what our simulations indicate," Donaldson said.

"Then your simulations are delusions."

"The Russians might interpret our delay as a gimmick. They'll think that we're waiting for the strike to respond—waiting for our wound, which will give us justification to lash back with everything we have."

"Mr. Donaldson, you're crazy, if you expect me to believe that."

"That doesn't make me wrong, Madam President."

MEANWHILE...

Brick emerged from the tunnel alone. No sign of Rodriguez.

I'll cover you.

Whatever that meant.

Brick stepped through the guardhouse and onto a lawn that was teeming with people, almost none of them in uniform.

Civilians?

No, not on the White House lawn. Couldn't be.

He pushed through the crowd, toward the Oval Office. Whose door was wide open. During a crisis. Not a single Marine sentry on duty.

His eyes must be blurry. Or perhaps, the sentries had discovered the perfect camouflage, one that made them completely invisible. That must be the answer. Because it was a hell of a lot more plausible than the idea of Marines vacating their most important post, anywhere on earth.

A rip of automatic gunfire, very close by. *Rat-tat-tat-tat.* An M240, a comforting sound, if ever he'd heard one. The Marines were still in the game. Just hiding behind cover, is all.

Brick went after the source of the noise. He was seconds away from his buddies. Everything would be okay.

Another burst of gunfire. For some reason, Brick hit the deck. Which was odd. As far as he could recall, he hadn't issued his body the order. This was no time for the ground. It was time to get into the action.

As he tried to get up his legs slipped on the grass. Very odd.

Slippery turf.

Another oddity: his hands were covered in blood. Had they been cut? No, they looked fine. They'd picked up the blood from somewhere else.

His stomach.

The dumb sons of bitches had shot him.

Maybe a bad wound, maybe not. No way to know.

More gunshots. People screaming, hitting the deck, collapsing.

A new thought occurred to Brick: Rodriguez had been manning the M240. He'd never pulled back. The crowd had overrun his position.

God help them all, if the intruders had gotten a weapon.

More shots. This was no time to rest. Not if the firepower belonged to the wrong side. Brick pulled himself off the ground and headed toward the West Wing.

11- MINUTES TO GO...

Abe couldn't take it anymore.

Maybe she had more important things to discuss. Responses and Black Books, and all the rest. But she couldn't face them. Not until covering what had to be on everybody's mind.

She turned to Sheridan's image. "You said we have two options for missile defense. What's the second?"

The general's face hadn't recovered from the miss. His jaw had rounded out a little; his hair had added a few grays.

Illusions, must be. People can't change in minutes.

Cities under bombardment, on the other hand...

"Our installation in Alaska," Sheridan said. "Fort Greely. They're firing as we speak."

"Prognosis?"

"We're having trouble with the system. I'm told we can only deploy a single interceptor at this time. In principle we should be okay. Our tests have passed more than they've failed. But the trajectory is tough. The weapon is coming in at an oblique angle; to hit it, we'll have to chase it down."

Abe put a hard pair of eyes on Sheridan's image. "Then why didn't you fire earlier?"

The general clenched his jaws. "As I said. Trouble with the system."

"Less than eleven minutes to impact," Colonel Patterson was saying.

How could these people keep going?

How could they bear not to run into a hole and hide?

"Madam President," Donaldson said. "I must tell you that every minute of delay increases the chance of further launches by the Russians."

"I don't even want to get into it," Abe said. "There's no way that could be true."

Donaldson went on, his voice even faster than before. "The Russians know that in the event of a random strike, US command will divide into multiple factions. One faction—moderates—will call for a concentrated strike, as per protocol. Another faction—hawks—will call for massive retaliation, protocol be damned. A strike against all targets. A third faction—doves—will call for nothing."

"I haven't..." Abe took up a water bottle and sipped away the dryness in her throat. "I haven't heard anyone call for retaliation."

"The Russians don't know that. But the instant we depart from protocol, they'll know the moderates have lost. So who won? Either the hawks or the doves. A flip of a coin. Nuclear powers don't risk their survival on the flip of a coin."

"Isn't that what we're doing? Betting everything on the hope that we guess right?"

"We shouldn't be guessing," Donaldson said.

"The Russians know it's the doves," Abe said. "We haven't launched yet."

"They'll know *nothing*. They'll think that the two sides are fighting each other. Do you think they'll trust the doves—the *weaklings*—to win? Bet their lives on it?"

"Will they risk the entire planet on the guess that we'll launch?"

"Will they risk their lives on the guess that we won't?" Donaldson jabbed a finger in Abe's direction. "If we don't follow protocol, the Russians will have no choice but to commit to a total response. No choice but to wipe us off the face of the earth."

(Thus the gods of simulation have decreed.)

10- MINUTES TO GO. . .

Abe said, "You're telling me that if we *don't* launch against the Russians, they'll respond more severely than if we *do*?"

Donaldson answered with a mirthless chuckle.

"That's insane," Abe said. "Which is why I'm starting to believe it."

"Welcome to the world we've inherited," Sheridan said.

Abe said, "When do we have to launch?"

Sheridan said, "Protocol tells us to launch as soon as possible, but no later than detonation, at which time primary command and control might be decapitated."

Abe felt a tap on her shoulder. A Secret Service agent. She looked up but barely saw him through the squalls of her mind.

"Ma'am," he said, "we have a problem."

"I'm working on it," she said.

"Not this one."

9+ MINUTES TO GO. . .

The Secret Service agent muttered something to Colonel Patterson, who hit a few keys on his laptop. A new image popped onto a wall screen. More security footage.

The first panel showed the White House wall. What was left of it. Lots of bodies, some resting on the ground, some scrambling over them.

No semblance of order.

The next showed the South Lawn: more bodies, vertical and horizontal. A number of the casualties appeared to be in uniform.

No semblance of order.

The next was the main building's entrance, its doors blown wide open, the crowd surging in.

Then, the interior. A succession of images. Shattered glass. Toppled furniture. Papers gently floating above the riotous mob. And bodies, more bodies, in each frame.

The crowd had managed to get inside.

"Freeze the picture," the agent said.

The chaos came to a blurry stop.

The agent stepped forward, withdrew a pen from his jacket, and placed it on an image of Cross Hall, the entrance hall. Normally the place was the picture of neoclassical serenity—white marble columns protecting busts of history's notables, a perfectly blood-red carpet fringed with gold. Now the busts were shattered and the carpet was charred. And covered with people.

The agent's pen was on a man, a very plainclothed man—jeans

and a thick coat—carrying what appeared to be an automatic rifle.

"This image is live," the agent said.

A new kind of unease introduced itself to the room: an immediate threat, directly upstairs.

"This is what happens when you incite a panic," Donaldson said.

Abe tried to brush that off. "How many casualties on the property?" she said.

"Impossible to know," the agent said. "Probably dozens. Maybe more."

Hundreds dead beyond the walls; dozens dead within the walls.

Already, the worst massacre ever on federal soil.

Put it on TV.

Not a good decision, Abe. Not good at all.

"Can they get down here?" Ed was saying.

"We can't afford to take that risk," the agent said.

"Madam President, I want you to know that I'm prepared to continue these proceedings in your absence," said a voice from the screen, one that had just appeared, one that Abe knew quite well. Too well.

Gerry Belman. VP for the previous administration. The man who had officially called Abe a "world-class idiot" and unofficially, a "second-rate bitch."

The man who for reasons of a *little stomach bug* was still the second-ranking official in the United States government, the one who'd make all the decisions should Abe fall out of the grid.

9 MINUTES TO GO. . .

The suits in the command center got ready to evacuate. Mutual looks, for reinforcement. Hands on arm rests, torsos tilted forward, waiting for the indication that it was okay to move.

Abe's face made it clear that it was not.

"Everyone sit," she said.

Nobody responded to that.

"Unless you all want to be fired," Abe said. "I suggest you sit."

They looked at each other, at the screen, at Abe. Slowly, the butts floated back down.

"Madam President," VP Belman said, "I know our administrations haven't exactly gotten along in the past, but I'm here to support you. In whatever way I can. I can manage things during your evacuation."

A seasoned veteran, directing the nation's response to a nuclear attack.

Not the worst option in the world.

Abe directed a question at the agent: "Where would we go?"

"Two options," the agent said. "North Tunnel and East. We've got bunkers in walking range of both exits, but neither one is very good for the present situation. Very limited communication capability…"

"How long to prepare our missiles?" she said.

"Two minutes," General Sheridan said.

"Two? I thought you said twenty-five."

"That's for the Russian missiles, which have to get pumped

with liquid propellants. Ours have solid rocket motors. Always fueled and ready to go."

"Ma'am," the agent was saying. "We must go now..."

"Ms. Armstrong," Secretary Donaldson was saying. "You should consider ordering our counterstrike prior to your evacuation. In case...we have trouble getting back in touch with you..."

"You needn't worry about that," the VP was saying. "I'll manage the process the way you want me to..."

"Less than nine minutes to go," Colonel Patterson was saying. "To have any chance of making it to the secondary bunker, you have to leave immediately..."

All those voices mixing into a soup. A thick, stinking, toxic soup.

Leave immediately.

Launch immediately.

Give up command, immediately.

The voices droned on. Red faces issuing their emphatic opinions. Abe's eyes fell on the face of the VP. Not such a bad face. Rather handsome in and older, pampered way. Thick head of gray hair, wide shoulders, nicely weathered skin. His appearance gave her the impression of a comfortable old sedan. Sturdy, American-made, and utterly impervious to redirection.

Subtly and mercifully, he was giving her an out. A way to recuse herself without embarrassment. She had to leave the bunker; the horde was at her gates. It was more than reasonable to delegate strike responsibility in her absence—to do anything else would be reckless. And of course she'd pass those responsibilities on to the VP. The second man in government, one who had orders of magnitude more experience on such matters.

A chance to stop being president during this awful experience. For a few minutes, at least.

Sounded like the best deal that was going to come her way.

8+ MINUTES TO GO. . .

"Ma'am," the agent said. "Now."

Abe began to rise, as much from relief as anything else. This wasn't her decision anymore.

But she never quite made it all the way up.

The truth came to her in a flash: leaving was itself a decision—a decision to pass command to a man who would, more than likely, follow protocol. He was a product of the system, maybe even an author of the system.

To leave this room was to validate a nuclear launch.

"I can't do this," she said. "I can't pass along the responsibility."

"Madam President," the VP said. "I assure you that in your absence, I'll follow your instructions. To the letter."

"What if something new develops while I'm away?"

"Such as?"

"A second launch. A declaration of war, by the Russians. An alien invasion. Anything."

The VP mulled it over. "I'd have to respond as I saw fit."

"Regardless of my orders?"

The VP didn't answer that.

How could she trust this man? He seemed nice enough, now that they weren't antagonists. But no matter what happened, things in the coming minutes were going to change. The ICBM would cross lines of latitude. The warheads would split up. The VP could use any of it to justify a comprehensive change of plans.

This was her show. Had been, ever since she'd taken that podium.

No way out of this one.

"Whoever wants to go can go," Abe said. "I'm staying."

The agent stepped forward. "Ma'am, that's out of the question."

"Don't tell me what's out of the question. Not today. I'm staying by the phone. I need to hear from our embassy."

"Madam President," the VP said, "We'd all feel much better if you were in a more secure location. I don't want to become your successor. Nobody wants me to, least of all my wife." He laughed without humor.

"It's my duty to see this through," Abe said. "All the way to the end. No interruptions."

"What happens if the crowd takes you?" Secretary Donaldson cut in. "Can you imagine—the president of the United States held hostage by a mob? What do you think that will do to the national character? You think they'll sit back and let the Russians get away with it?"

"Mr. Donaldson, we have no idea of the Russians' intentions."

"They'll be out for blood. They'll demand we hit the Russians with everything we have."

Abe's thoughts rose to the ground overhead. A stampede clobbering the artifacts of the presidency, overturning statues, toppling file cabinets, tearing apart documents that took generations to build.

She'd never worked in that space. The mob had gotten there before she had.

She couldn't clear them away, wasn't even sure if she still had the manpower. But even if she did, it was a bad option. Killing to protect property. She couldn't do that.

But killing to retain order, that she'd have to get used to.

She pointed to the Secret Service agent. "Tell your men to secure the West Wing by all means necessary. West Wing only. The crowd can have the rest of the property. Something tells me it'll be a long time before a president works above ground."

"What about the documents?" the agent said. "The computers?"

"Forget about them." She glared at Secretary Donaldson. "The Russians already have our secrets anyway."

7 MINUTES TO GO...

On the map, the older, inert yellow line had gained a twin, one that was stretching to the southeast, looking to merge into the ICBM's lane rather than slam head on.

The backup option, playing catchup.

Impossibly, it was actually gaining. Abe's heart skipped a beat. The ICBM was going four miles per second; who knew how fast the intercept missile was flying. Perhaps this shot would be easier—would require more power to arrive but have a better chance of connecting once it got there. It's easier to sideswipe a car than smash it head-on.

Was it as effective?

"Still no word from the Moscow embassy," General Sheridan said. "No cellphones, no landlines."

"How long does it take to wipe a couple of hard drives?" Abe said.

"Not that long," Donaldson said. "It has to be something else."

"You think they've been overrun?" Abe said.

"They would have hit the alarm. Takes a quarter of a second."

"Then what do you think happened?"

"Fire sale," Donaldson said.

Abe blinked at him. "I don't follow."

"Fire sale cyber attack. Everything goes. Like an EMP written by programmers."

"You mean a computer virus?"

"I mean a computer plague."

7- MINUTES TO GO. . .

On the map, the yellow line seemed to be speeding up. This interceptor was pissed off. It was going to do its duty. Abe was sure of it.

Back to the conversation. She said, "You think the Russians have been hit with a virus?"

"I don't have a clue," Secretary Donaldson said. "But I can't think of another reason they'd go silent, together with our embassy."

"It's exactly as I said earlier," Abe said. "All of this could be a virus. Our blip could be nothing more than a computer fantasy."

General Sheridan said, "All but impossible. It's one thing to disrupt a computer system, another to fool it into seeing things. The difference between knocking someone out and implanting him with visions."

"But you can implant hallucinations," Abe said. "You can brainwash people."

"Not our people," was all Donaldson replied. He seemed to be distracted. Like nearly everybody else in the room, his eyes were on the door.

As if they all expected a mob to rush in any second.

MEANWHILE. . .

The weather shifted in the West Wing.

As Brick looked on, a thick cloud rolled forward, snuffing out the corridor's features.

No indication of its source. Could be a fire. Could be a biological attack.

Could be completely irrelevant.

He donned a gas mask just as the first vapors enveloped him. He paused for a quick whiff. He couldn't resist. Instantly coughed the thing up.

Teargas, gunpowder and smoke.

From dead reckoning, he knew that he was just south of the hall leading to the bunker, but he couldn't see its elevator. The fog made a haze of the world around him. He could barely make out the signs on the wall. Certainly couldn't see any other Marines.

Where the hell were the squads?

Was *he* the only squad?

His belly was on fire. He'd never inspected the wound. Either it was fatal or it wasn't. His mission hadn't changed: no unauthorized persons could go downstairs.

A face emerged from the cloud. A civilian, an undershirt wrapped below eyes so red they'd probably cry blood. No mask on that guy.

And even so he was pressing on.

A single turn would bring that man to the bunker. A prohibited area, if ever there were one. That wasn't going to happen.

Brick caught the man by the shoulders and threw him to the floor. The man was ready for a fight. Scrambled to his feet and tried to tackle Brick by the legs. Brick kicked him back and warned him away with his rifle.

Another man flashed into view, making Brick officially outnumbered. Time to escalate the response. He drew back his rifle to butt the man in the face, but stopped when he recognized the features.

Horn-rimmed glasses, narrow face, wispy hair.

This was Jason Harper, secretary of state under the prior administration. His hands were up.

"Sorry sir," Brick said. He lowered his weapon.

The secretary didn't lower his hands.

"I know who you are," Brick said. "You should come with me, sir. We need to get you in the open air."

Brick moved toward the closest exit.

The secretary didn't follow.

He had a funny look on his face. Something almost like a grin, only much more fearful.

Brick was about to ask what was wrong, but a thinning of the fog answered the question for him.

The secretary had a gun to his back. An M240 with "INSTANT JUSTICE" stenciled on the stock.

Rodriguez's weapon.

The gunman was a compact guy with short brown hair and a face that said he'd already been through a war.

"We know it's down that hall," the gunman said.

He was talking about the bunker. The world was a whitewash. Visibility five feet. There could be any number of guys standing behind the gunman.

"We're all dead when the bomb goes off," the gunman said. "You should go down there with us."

"Nobody goes downstairs," Brick said. "Drop you're weapon and I promise I'll help you."

"I'm going to shoot this guy."

"You picked the wrong hostage."

The gunman scoffed. "This is the secretary of state."

"Which means he's not the president. Which means he's not getting within a hundred feet of that bunker. And neither are you."

"Marine, step aside," the secretary said.

Brick shook his head. "I can't do that, sir."

"Fine," the gunman said. "Then I will."

The barrel swung over. Cleared the secretary's back. Stared Brick down for a fraction of a second.

His friend's gun.

I'll cover you.

Brick had only enough time for the briefest pang of regret before the barrel flashed and the world snapped away.

6† MINUTES TO GO. . .

The command center talked so fast its words overlapped.

Sheridan said, "The window is closing. You *must* make a decision."

Something had changed. As the deadline approached the room had lost its formality. Its respect. No ma'ams, anymore. No *Madam Presidents.* Just *you.*

Abe said, "I'm not ready."

"Will you ever be?" Donaldson said.

"I don't have enough information."

"I do," Donaldson said. "Let me make it."

Abe shook her head. "That would be a decision."

"We need your leadership."

"I've already given it."

Donaldson scoffed. "By sending out the emergency notice, and then lowering your guns against the ensuing mob. How has that turned out?"

Abe didn't answer.

"When you drop your guns," Donaldson said, "people die."

"They also die when you shoot," Abe said.

"They die either way," General Sheridan cut in.

The gravity of his voice, the abruptness with which he said it— it was clear he wasn't simply responding to the conversation. He was saying something different. He had new information.

He explained: "Our second interceptor has failed."

A great mass shifted out of the room. Abe hadn't known it was there until it was gone. A lingering hope, that this nightmare was nothing more than that: a horror from which they would soon awake.

But there was no awakening now. No more response measures. No more yellow lines.

The map kept charting the path of the failed intercept. Showed the yellow line falling behind the red one.

But no—it wasn't just *one* red line anymore. It had forked.

"The reentry vehicles have split apart," Sheridan was saying. "We now have confirmation of their targeting. Boston, New York City, and Washington. And we have no ability to intercept them."

MEANWHILE. . .

Secretary Halder looked on in shock. The bullet-riddled body of the slain Marine lay oozing at his feet. Said a little prayer. Cursed himself for not coming up with a plan. Something that would have saved the man's life.

At first the secretary hadn't believed the gunman capable of murder. He believed it now.

The gun nudged his back. The same gun that had just killed a man.

"Move it," said the gunman, behind him.

He wanted Halder to continue down the hall, toward the bunker. Halder couldn't blame him. The air in here was toxic. Barely enough to survive, let alone think.

The secretary got moving, stopped at a black door. Wooden frame, brass handle. Totally unremarkable, by design.

"You'd better not be playing games," the gunman said.

"You're a civilian with a weapon," Halder said. "They're not going to let you down there. Not in a million years."

"You don't have a million years, old man. Open that door or you're going to wind up like the other guy. I promise."

The doors wouldn't simply open, of course. You had to push aside a little painting. A sailboat on a placid bay. The little enclosure behind it held a keypad.

Six digits, well known to Halder. He'd attended a handful of drills over the past two years. When you get this notice, go here; when you get that, go there. Most roads led downstairs.

He should have come here first, before the chaos.

He could have helped the president.

Could have helped that dead Marine.

Now he didn't have a choice. If he left the gunman here, the latter would find another Marine. Kill another Marine.

All the man wanted was shelter. Anybody in his position would want the same thing.

The gun jabbed again.

No choice in the matter. The secretary had to do it.

The president wasn't really in danger. One look at that gun, and the Secret Service would bring this standoff to a quick and permanent conclusion.

A few taps on the code panel, and the elevator doors swung open.

Fresh air rushed out. Delicious air.

This was a false alarm. Had to be. Harper knew President Yakushev well, knew the leader of the Strategic Rocket Forces, even knew Admiral Sharapov, leader of the demonstrations. Cold men, to be sure. And calculating. But reasonable. They'd happily trample an enemy, but never one who possessed the means to destroy them.

This would be over soon.

And sooner for the gunman than he knew.

Together, the two men stepped into the elevator. The panel was glowing red: agents had barred the elevator from moving. It wouldn't do for an invader to drop in on them while they planned the end of the world.

But Harper wasn't an invader. He had the override code.

He punched it in and listened to the sweet sounds of the elevator motors whirling into action. The sweet sounds of his own salvation.

MEANWHILE. . .

The agent watched a security screen as two men mounted the elevator to the bunker.

Quite a conundrum, but one within the agent's control. His finger was on a switch, one that would override any instructions the men in the elevator entered.

And the agent would have flicked that switch, for almost any visitors in the world. But one of the men was a notable, to say the least, and by the look of it he was in great peril.

A conundrum indeed.

The agent picked up his phone. The other end rang for quite some time before cutting off.

Apparently his superiors had more important things to do.

He tried again, and this time the other side picked up. But it was too late. The secretary of state was already on his way down.

A gunman, in the presidential bunker. Today brought no end to the surprises.

The agent hit a button, signaling a breach of the bunker.

6 MINUTES TO GO. . .

The ceiling went red.

Abe said, "Is that some kind of a—has the weapon landed?"

"No," Donaldson said. "Looks more like a fire alarm."

A Secret Service agent appeared in the doorway. "We have a breach in the bunker," he said. "The gunman from Cross Hall."

Abe turned to the security footage, still frozen on the man's image. The pixelation of the screen magnified his grimace. Made his face a study in desperation.

A veteran of a brand new war. A nuclear war.

"He's in the bunker?" Abe said.

"The elevator," the agent said. "He's taken the former secretary of state hostage."

Halder. Not a bad man, certainly not by the standards of the previous administration.

"What does he want?" Abe said.

"It doesn't matter, ma'am. He's not getting it."

"And he's going to kill Halder?"

"There's no reason for alarm," the agent said. "In a few moments, this will all be over."

The edge in the agent's voice suggested that Halder's fate might not end up so different from the gunman's.

The Secret Service were going to keep the bunker secure, no matter the collateral damage.

More deaths on Abe's watch.

"Everyone stay here," she said.

She stepped out.

MEANWHILE...

The elevator doors whisked open silently, confidently. No ding. No music.

The secretary of state appeared ramrod-straight, his head turned slightly to the side, as though he couldn't stand the sight of what was in front of him.

For good reason. He was facing a dozen guns.

"Drop your weapon," one of the agents said.

The gunman behind the secretary of state didn't move. "People are dying upstairs. My...wife...You did it. You told us to run but didn't give us any place to go."

"Drop your weapon."

The man jabbed the secretary's back with the rifle. "I just want to come in. I don't want to hurt anybody. It's hell, topside."

"Sir," the agent said, "if you don't drop that weapon we will be forced to shoot you."

"I don't want to shoot anybody. I just want a promise you won't hurt me."

"This is your last warning. Under no circumstances will we allow you to step off that elevator with a gun."

The secretary was trembling. He wasn't the target of those guns, but he was only inches away. In a standoff. A shootout would be nearly as dangerous for him as the gunman behind him.

Things were about to take a turn for the worse when a clamor broke out behind the assembled agents. Secretary Halder craned his neck to have a look. A new threat?

In a sense, perhaps it was. For there, not twenty feet from the elevator that held a machine gun-toting refugee, stood the president of the United States.

6- MINUTES TO GO. . .

"Get her out of here!"

The agents couldn't have drawn a tighter circle around the president if they'd been cinched together with rope. Hands seized all of her limbs, arms and legs, and hoisted her off the floor. Ushered her back to the safety of the hall.

She squirmed, snapped out of the grips, threw up her hands and pushed the agents back.

"Ma'am," one of the agents said, "you can't stay here."

"I can't go," she said.

She cautioned him back with her eyes. Let him know that she might be far smaller, far weaker, but she was still the president of the United States, and this was an emergency, and anybody who stood in her way was about to find out how she planned to use her emergency powers.

The agents stepped aside.

She stepped forward.

Plenty of confusion in that lobby. Nobody understood her purpose. The agents allowed her to move, but they moved with her, like the membrane around the nucleus of a cell.

When the membrane was within ten feet of the elevator it stopped. Abe stepped forward and put her hands on the shoulders of two agents, silently instructing them to part.

"He's right there, ma'am," they said, with voices as tight as drums.

"I know. Step aside, gentlemen."

They did as instructed. Abe stepped forward and saw the anxious face of the secretary of state, his eyes the color of cherries, his nose and mouth caked in mucus. He was panting. Behind him, almost totally concealed, was another man. A huge gun.

Guns everywhere.

Stress hormones filled the room like an invisible gas. One spark, one provocation, and everything was going to explode. Abe had never felt so powerfully that mankind is an animal. More intelligent and self-aware, most of the time. But an animal, endowed with a killing instinct that dated back to the chemical combat of life's protoplastic soup.

She stepped forward again. Hands stronger than vices took hold of her arms. They'd let her go no further, no matter her orders.

Fine. She could do her business from here.

"They want me to launch," she said.

The former secretary of state responded: "Are you telling me this is real—"

"I'm not talking to you," she said. "I'm talking to the citizen behind you."

The gunman answered with a breathless voice. "How do you know I'm a…a citizen?"

"You seem to support the Second Amendment. I need to talk with you, but I can't do that when you're holding a gun. Will you drop it?"

"They'll shoot me."

"I won't let them. I don't have much time. Drop your gun."

"Not until you promise to let more people into the bunker."

"Out of the question."

"It's war up there. People are dying."

"This is the command center, sir. I can't have chaos down here."

"First let me tell you what I want—"

"I AM THE PRESIDENT OF THE UNITED STATES. DROP THE FUCKING GUN."

The man didn't move. His face was slick with sweat. His clothes were in tatters. He looked like he'd been through a tour in an ugly part of the world. That descriptor now fit Washington, if it fit anywhere.

His gun swung into view. A new wave of tension washed over the agents. Abe could almost hear their fingers tightening over the triggers.

Then the man removed his strap and threw the thing onto the floor.

An agent rushed forward to retrieve it.

"Step out from behind the secretary of state and put up your arms," Abe said to the gunman. "No one will harm you. Agents, please keep your hands off this man."

The man complied. His face was smeared with an untold mixture of fluids, some bodily, some not. His eyes were hemorrhaging. The effects of pepper spray, no doubt. He was wearing a thick coat, but even so he was shaking.

"Were you attending the inauguration?" she said.

A stir behind her, then a voice. Donaldson's. "Madam President, we have to—"

"Just a minute," she said, not removing her eyes from the gunman. "Were you attending the inauguration?"

"Yes," the gunman said.

"Did you vote for me?"

"No."

She smiled. "Then there's no doubting your judgment. They…" She jutted her chin at Donaldson. "…want me to launch our nukes."

"When?"

"Now."

"How many?"

"Forty."

"Jesus. How many are coming at us?"

"One missile, three warheads."

"Jesus."

"We haven't heard from the Russians. Have no idea what they're up to."

"Jesus."

"What should I do?" Abe said.

The man paused a beat. "How long to decide?"

"Less than six minutes until the bombs hit us."

"Less than *five* minutes," Donaldson said.

"What should I do?" Abe repeated.

The gunman licked his lips. Flicked his eyes between the president and her secretary of defense. He almost seemed to relish the moment. Nuclear war or no, it isn't every day the commanders of history's mightiest war machine solicit your advice.

"Nuke them," the gunman said. "Biggest nukes we've got."

"You want to start a nuclear war?" Abe said.

"Sounds like the Russians already started it. So we have to finish it. When somebody punches you, you've got to knock them out. Worst thing in the world is to let them punch you again."

Abe nodded. "Take this man to a comfortable room."

"He murdered someone," Secretary Halder announced. "A Marine."

A sad story, but one that had played out a thousand times in the wake of her decision.

The only decision she could have made.

It was time to get used to it.

"Then make sure the room has a lock," Abe said. She wove through the agents. "And for God's sake, keep that elevator down here."

4 MINUTES TO GO...

"I don't know what the hell you were thinking," Donaldson said as he resumed his seat.

"I caused the problem," Abe said as she took hers. "It was mine to fix."

"And if the fix had killed you?"

"It didn't."

"Glad to see you back," Sheridan said. His face made it clear he meant it. "What's the call?"

Abe scanned the room's faces. All weary, all anxious, all turned to the map on screen. The red lines were now over the southern arm of the Hudson Bay.

Back to the faces. Some fear on them, but remarkably little. These men and women had families topside, most in Washington. They were about to lose husbands, wives, and children.

Had they had time to say goodbye?

No. They'd spent the vast bulk of the past half hour waiting for her to do what the people had elected her to do.

"Have we heard from the Moscow embassy?" she said.

"No word," Sheridan said. "It's as I said. We'll have to make the decision with the information already in our possession."

What information was that?

Three red lines stretching across a black map. The words of a general, promising that those lines represented the genuine flight of more firepower than had been unleashed in any other attack in history. Promising that this wasn't a fluke. That the Russians' silence was likely the result of a computer *plague,* one that had incapacitated all of their electronics—but that hadn't so much as scratched our detection network. No, that wasn't possible. The Russians' machines were going haywire, but ours were just fine, thank you. Made in the USA, back when we built things to last.

Fire against the launch site, the protocol said.

Hit them with twenty good, old-fashioned megatons.

The gunman, standing in the elevator like a refugee from the apocalypse: "Nuke them. Everything we've got. Biggest nukes we've got. When somebody punches you, you've got to knock them out."

The general had spoken.

And the *people* had spoken.

That was all the information Abe was ever going to get.

She tore open the football, withdrew the Black Book, and discussed a new set of options.

4 - MINUTES TO GO. . .

Abe's lungs trembled as she spoke into the bunker's secure link. She had no idea if she was doing the right thing.

No, strike that—she knew it was a terrible thing to do. But it was less terrible than every alternative.

She hoped.

She said, "I hereby authorize a nuclear strike. Mike—November—Yankee…."

A long string of alphanumerics followed. Sheridan listened with his mouth agape.

"Ma'am," he said, "there's been a mistake."

"No mistake," Abe said. "Colonel Patterson has provided the targeting. He's with the Air Force. They don't make mistakes."

"We've never discussed that attack profile," Sheridan said. "We've probably never even simulated it."

Nuke them. Biggest nukes we've got.

Donaldson didn't move. Like everyone else in the room, and on the screens, he seemed to have contracted sudden paralysis. Abe had seen photographs with more movement.

"Mr. Donaldson," Abe said. "Please authenticate my—"

Donaldson cut in: "I can't do that, Madam President."

His voice wasn't insubordinate; it was plaintive, almost whimpering. He was drowning in confusion. Utterly overwhelmed.

Welcome to the club.

"This doesn't mean you agree with me," Abe said. "You're not liable for my order. You just have to tell the secure link that you heard it from my lips."

Donaldson was sweating. "That's easier said than done."

"We don't have a lot of time," Abe said.

"Do you have any idea what the Russians will do when they see those nukes go up? They'll know we're not following protocol. Probably think we're launching against Moscow—which is what their tracking will show. They'll respond with everything they have. The whole arsenal. Thousands of warheads. Not a single American city will be left. Not a single—"

Donaldson's last word was lost to a choke.

There was some truth to what he'd said. It was possible that the Russians would mistake this as an attack on their biggest cities. That they'd respond by wiping America off the planet. That it would be the last order given by a president of the United States, ever.

But it was certain, that it was the only order Abe could give.

She despised Donaldson. Despised a world that conceived of weapons that extinguished millions as easily as a porch light. And most of all, she despised herself for fighting with all her mind, body and soul to win the right to place her finger on the button.

Then she breathed it all away. In and out. Found a strange calmness settling over her, not out of a newfound confidence, not out of the sense that things would be okay—but out of desperation to put this behind her.

She slid her chair toward Donaldson. Touched his shoulder. Made human contact, the very element that had been programmed out of the nuclear chain of command. Spoke in a calm, commanding, reassuring voice. Her mother's voice.

Her mother, way out there in the middle of flyover country.

Watching it all on TV.

"I don't envy you, Mr. Donaldson," she said. "The weight of the world is on your shoulders. No matter how you decide, people are going to die. But on one hand you can follow my instructions, and allow the blame to go to me. Or you can disobey my instructions. Force an entirely different response to the Russian launch. Maybe you can even convince Sheridan to execute the protocol. Let loose our twenty megatons. But then you'll have to live with history's judgment. Forty ICBMs streaking across the Russian radar screens. A nuclear war, of your own making. Can you live with that? Do you want to be the one who decides whether our kids are going to grow up? Is that fair to you? Is it what you signed up for?"

Donaldson broke eye contact. Stared at his hands, braced against the table, as though preparing for a great cataclysm from behind. Lost what little color his face had ever possessed.

The sound of a clock ticking. Of papers fluttering in the breeze from the air conditioning vent. Of agents quietly conferring in the hallway.

The following second stretched into a minute, an hour, a day. By Abe's internal clock, anyway.

Then Donaldson turned to General Sheridan's image.

"General, I hereby authenticate the president's order. Mike—November…"

Abe didn't bother with a feeling of relief. Relief was preposterous, at a time like this.

She stood and looked at the colonel. "Advise the general of the…arming priorities, as you call them. And give me the map. Something portable."

The colonel handed Abe a tablet, its display dark but for the red lines of the warheads. She went to the doorway.

"Call your families," she said to the room. "We're done here."

"That's it?" Donaldson said. "What if your plan fails?"

"If it fails," Abe said, "then there's no need for this room."

She stepped out.

2+ MINUTES TO GO. . .

Abe found Jim in a bedroom the size of a walk-in closet. He sat on a gunmetal gray cot, listening to a radio stuffed with vacuum tubes.

When he saw her he started.

"I didn't feel like watching the TV in the lounge," he said. "This thing has better speakers."

It sounded like a tin can.

Jim stood up, and she fell into his arms. Closed her eyes and tried to squeeze the air out of him.

"Are you okay?" he said.

"I don't know."

She broke away, propped the tablet on the desk and sat with him on the edge of the mattress.

"Would you still love me if I ended the world?" she said.

"Definitely."

"If I made out with the vice president?"

"Ingoing or out?"

"Both."

"That's against my orders, Armstrong." He smiled.

"Do you know what's happened?"

He nodded and pointed to the radio, still squawking. "Plugged directly into the command center. Benefit of being buddies with the Secret Service."

"You hardly know the Secret Service."

"Even better. Honeymoon period."

"Honeymoon period," Abe said. "This is my honeymoon

period." She gestured at the room around them. "Bunkers and bombs. Nukes flying overhead."

"It's not your fault."

"We missed it, Jim. Two attempts at interception. Two failures."

"It's *not* your fault. Don't put this on yourself."

"You should have seen me in that room. I had no idea what was going on. Couldn't decide anything."

"You did great." He ran a hand through her hair. "Not that I know what you're doing."

"That makes two of us."

"You fired back?"

Abe nodded. "But only at us."

She'd launched, alright. But not at the Russians.

She'd sent her nukes into the sky.

It just so happened, the navy had a third of its subs off the Atlantic Coast. War exercise. She'd ordered them to fire a series of tactical nuclear missiles, to blast the incoming bombs out of the sky.

It wouldn't be clean. It would fry all electronics between Boston and Miami. But it would save them.

If they got lucky.

If her decision was sound.

Decisions…today, she'd learned a great deal on the subject. For a president, information is almost impossible to come by. Good information, anyway. No advisers can ever know the full truth; and what tiny piece of the puzzle they do possess passes through a tortuous gauntlet of prejudices, inhibitions and misjudgments before finally reaching their mouths.

Decisions at the presidential level will always rely as much on instinct as they do on research. The bigger the decision, the greater the need for instinct.

Today's had come purely from the gut.

And she'd learned something else, a secret buried miles beneath the silos: it is insane to launch a nuclear weapon against human flesh.

Period. In all circumstances. No matter what the protocols say.

So what if you destroy the enemy? It's impossible to celebrate victory when you're dead.

The tablet now showed three red lines silently tracing south, not too far from Toronto. Two minutes from impact, but still over another country.

"It doesn't feel real," Jim said.

"Wait a few minutes."

"Then it'll feel even less real."

"I didn't know what to do, Jim."

"Lie down with me."

"I just didn't know. Maybe if I'd have paid more attention to the briefings, if I'd had a few chats with Yakushev, I…I thought it was over. The Cold War, I mean. I never thought the Russians would launch."

Jim rubbed her arm. "Lie down with me."

"*Nobody* thought they would launch. That's the most insane part of this whole thing. The system was designed to make sure nobody would use it."

Jim didn't respond. He wrapped an arm around her waist, brushed away her hair, kissed her on the cheek.

Back to the tablet. New lines had appeared, blue ones. The good guys. Abe's legacy. If the world had legacies anymore.

Those lines grew, pixel by pixel.

1 MINUTE TO GO...

The last of the red warheads crossed the border into the United States.

Jim leaned back and pulled Abe's body into his. His hands were trembling. His heart was battering her ribs. His breaths were quick.

So were hers.

She pushed back a little more, cupping herself into his body. His arm was over her waist; she took his hand in both of hers and brought it to her chest. Cuddled the big mitt like a teddy bear.

They didn't speak.

They didn't look at the screen.

Abe heard the whir of the air conditioning system, fed by tanks that had been filled long ago, perhaps during the Cold War. Fitting. To breathe ancient air while awaiting destruction by ancient weapons.

Would they hear it, all the way down here?

Would they feel it?

Jim's breaths came fast and shallow, but reassuring all the same. She knew he wanted to comfort her but didn't know how. A good man. Too smart to persist with cliché—*this isn't your fault; you did great; maybe next time, honey.*

Too smart to ignore that the next few seconds would expose his lies.

SECONDS TO GO. . .

As the lines approached and the seconds danced Jim pulled her tighter.

Abe twisted and hugged him back.

They lay for what seemed in those endless seconds like quite a while. Heads locked like their bodies, breaths tickling each other's ears.

They gnashed each other's ribs. Held as tightly as they could. Braced themselves against nuclear winds that would try to yank them apart.

In the final seconds a tremble passed between them. Their bodies answered to the same panicked command.

Abe swallowed and licked her lips, brushing away a dryness fed by stale air. She drew them to his ear, close enough to feel it. She breathed in, heard the whistle of ingoing air across his skin.

She closed her eyes. "I love you."

He didn't respond. Because by then, everything had gone dark.

SECONDS LATER. . .

Admiral Sharapov, tall, paunchy and exhausted, huddled over the shoulder of a young console operator deep in the bowels of Russian Missile Command.

"Their warheads have detonated, sir," said the young man.

The admiral was sure he'd misheard.

"That's impossible," he said. "They couldn't have even cleared American airspace by now."

"Somebody must have hit the self-destruct." The youth sounded sheepish, almost apologetic. As if this were his fault.

There was a clamor, behind the admiral. Through the swells of his mind he barely noticed.

"Americans aren't fools," he said. "Their missiles don't self-destruct. They go exactly where they're targeted."

Sharapov's formidable mind was racing, and not in a good direction.

"What about our warheads?" he said. "Have they detonated?"

The youth hit up another screen but said nothing.

The disturbance behind them was growing louder.

"Well?" the admiral said. "Have they blown up?"

"No evidence of detonation," the youth said. "I don't know what happened to them."

It wasn't hard for the admiral to figure out, and when he did his stomach dropped to his feet.

The Americans had used their warheads to shoot his down. Had in seconds destroyed the plans of a decade. A career.

It had been foolish of him to strike during the inauguration. Yes, there should have been more confusion. More immaturity. A greater chance of manipulating the inexperienced American administration into responding as Sharapov intended.

But it was now clear that the last president would have been better. He was a bellicose man. He would have fired back at the launch site, as dictated by American protocol.

A day earlier, all of this would have worked.

One day.

But perhaps not all was lost.

"Dead Hand," the admiral said, "will it still trigger a counterstrike?"

"Not if their missiles fail to reach our airspace. And I see no indication of further launches. I think the Americans are waiting for our next move, sir."

The admiral wobbled on his feet. He'd caused a little chaos in his country. Had clogged Moscow with riots, had shut down the country's networks, had even managed to hijack a single missile silo. But all of that was temporary. Only a nuclear exchange with the Americans could have given him the cover he needed to seize Russia for good and rebuild her as he saw fit.

But the Americans had denied him such an exchange.

The noise behind him reached a deafening pitch, and then a blast door blew open. Soldiers stormed in. The very soldiers who'd promised to support him until the very end.

But then again this was the end, premature though it may be. In a desperate attempt to clear themselves, they were switching over to the other side. Undoubtedly they'd proclaim their innocence as they frog-marched him to the Kremlin.

The traitors.

A navy man should never have trusted the Strategic Rocket Forces. That had been a mistake.

And it was time for someone to pay.

He drew the pistol at his side and pointed it at the youth's face.

If he didn't have a country's fate in his hands, at least he had the youth's.

The boy looked up anxiously. Clenched his jaws. Swallowed. He was terrified, but he made no attempt to plead for his life.

He was braver than most. Perhaps he didn't deserve to die.

Which didn't mean everyone got a pass. Failure should have consequences.

In a quick movement, Sharapov brought the gun about and stuck it in his own mouth.

The very mouth that was supposed to give the rousing speeches that were to dig Russia out of her nuclear catastrophe. That would have won him a place among the giants. Ivan the Formidable. Peter the Great. Stalin.

Oh well. Not everyone can win.

He angled the gun upwards, toward the most vital parts of his own body. Took a long last breath.

And as the youth looked on, the admiral pulled the trigger.

A humble request

Reviews are everything in this business. I'm deeply grateful for every one I get. They don't have to be long. A few words from a few people can make all the difference. If you'd like to see more of my work, please consider leaving one.

About the author

Zach Kraft is the author of numerous novels, including *The Counting* series. More about his work can be found at www.ZachKraft.com.

A sneak peak

Turn the page for a look at Book 1 in *The Counting* series of novels:

Counting the Ones We Kill

one

I got in trouble when I didn't celebrate the abduction of my family.

There's an event you're supposed to go to. The goodbye party. It's at the Ministry of Election, better known as the M.O.E. Your family isn't there, of course. They're gone for good. But you're supposed to bring something you can send off. Little talismans. Photos, socks, even toiletries. I heard of one guy who brought a used tissue. His son had allergies. Most people find that touching. I always get sick when I think about it.

I thought about it a lot the day of my goodbye party. I couldn't even get out of bed. I considered what it would be like, going through my daughter's room, opening drawers, staring at old notes, old drawings.

What would I choose? That was the hardest part. I'd have to go through everything and find something to sum up her life. Something to say goodbye to. I think I could run a three-minute mile, before I could do that.

You aren't allowed to say goodbye in person. Because it's not really goodbye. That's what the Bugs say, or at least their mouthpieces at the M.O.E. When your wife gets the honor, when the tread tank pulls up to your house while you're out chasing your latest client's demons, they don't offer her a call. She's not a criminal, they say. She doesn't need one. They pack her in and drive off.

And maybe, if you're lucky enough, they'll also do it to your daughter on that very same day.

I hit the jackpot, as far as the Bugs are concerned.

Are the two of them together? Your guess is better than mine. For all I know, they took my wife to one end of the universe and my daughter to the opposite end. But I like to think they're together. Probably complaining about me. Gossiping. Maybe they think of it as a vacation. Girls' decade out.

But it hasn't been a decade. Only four years.

Four years is longer than you think.

Life goes on. That's what everybody says. You have to move through the days and pretend everything is normal. Go back to work. Make sure you get enough to eat. Three squares a day, whether you feel like it or not.

And most importantly, shut your mouth about what happened. Because it's an honor to be Elected, not a tragedy. Your family is fine. They're zipping across the galaxies, or perhaps even flipping through the multiverse. The Bugs are rumored to do that. They don't live with our limitations.

Or maybe they're dead. Your departed family, I mean. We're not supposed to speculate about this, but I can't help it. Some days I *hope* they're dead. It's better than living with the Bugs.

But I had to live with them, even if our relationship wasn't so good. I hadn't attended the goodbye bonanza. I didn't put on my party hat and blow my noisemaker and eat stale cake. I stayed in bed. So they weren't happy with me.

They didn't say anything, of course. They never do. They sit up there in the sky, watching us. Judging us. Planning what to do next.

two

I don't sleep as well as I used to. I have this worry. Or maybe it's a fantasy. Maybe it's both.

Here's how it goes. I get a call in the middle of the night. A grainy video of my daughter will show up on my ceiling screen. She'll tell me she's in trouble, needs my help. I respond that I'll find a way to get to her. Even if she's in a different universe, I'll find a way.

Nobody's ever gotten a call like that, but I know I will. My kid is different. One of these nights it's coming, and I can't miss it.

Turns out, this whole mess began when my ceiling blinked on in the middle of the night. You can imagine how I took that. I almost had a heart attack. I tore off the sheets and started to get dressed even before the image resolved.

But it wasn't a blond kid with a messy bob. Not even close. Instead, I got two bloodshot eyes and a red light of a nose. Captain Meynard.

I had to sit on my bed and collect myself.

"Everything okay?" he said.

"I just—" I rubbed my face. "I thought you were someone

else."

"You get a lot of calls on the Em?" Em: Emergency Link.

Not where it counted, I didn't.

"What can I do for you?" I said.

"We've got a stiff."

I'm a private cop, not a public one, but Meynard calls me for help from time to time. Those times were getting fewer and farther between. The Bugs didn't want him to work with me anymore.

I said, "Put it on ice and call me in the morning."

"Don't kid around. This one's a sad case."

Truth is, they're all sad cases. Cops don't officiate weddings and bar mitzvahs. But the way he said it, the peculiar feeling in his voice, made me drop the sarcasm. Something was different about this one.

Who knew? Even I can be right occasionally.

He told me to meet him at the Pit. I tried to hide the anxiety in my voice when I said okay.

We don't understand too much about the Bugs. We don't know what they look like, where they came from, why they chose earth.

Even the name *Bugs* is a mystery. We all picture them as seven-foot praying mantises. Big eyes and lanky limbs. But we have no reason to think that. They've never stepped out of their crafts, the gigantic tubes that hover over our cities like metal clouds.

When they arrived, they took the first of the Elect and trained them to be their representatives on earth. All we know about our alien overlords is what comes from the mouths of the people who serve them. May God bless the M.O.E.

The Pit was one of the Bugs' first construction projects. Great jaws dropped out of the sky and chewed up the earth, in the center of Sun City. They'd given us several minutes' advanced notice, of course. So no more than a few thousand died that day. When they were done they'd left a crater a mile wide and nearly as deep. Nobody knew why.

It was as if the Bugs had found a malignancy in the earth and decided to excise it with plenty of margin.

I don't particularly care for the idea of recreating in a bottomless pit, so I generally stay away from the place. I certainly didn't relish the idea of traipsing there alone, in the middle of the night.

At least they made it easy for me to get in.

A helmeted guard met me at the fence. Not that I care for helmets. They make it impossible to know if I'm dealing with a man or a machine. The cynics say there isn't a difference, but I'm not ready to accept that. I wasn't ready at that time, anyway.

He checked my ID, opened a gate and gestured me through. I walked in slowly, because I had no idea what to expect. For a few steps I caught something: ruins, as of an ancient city. Fallen arches, collapsed columns, even statues, their faces big as houses. Some of them were human, some were vastly different from human. Yet they were familiar. Strikingly familiar…

A row of lights burst into life, blinding me. A voice cried out:
STAY ON THE RED LINE, PLEASE.

It took a dozen blinks to see a glowing red arrow that led off into the distance. They wanted me to follow a narrow path.

Time being, I was okay with that.

The crime scene was lit up like the skies of a city under aerial bombardment. Two full batteries of floodlights, one circling the other. Meynard stood behind them, a wrinkly trench coat wrapped over his sloppy bulk, a cup of coffee in one hand and a cigarette in the other.

I took the cup, thanked him, drained it in a gulp.

"That's mine," he said.

"Well in that case." I handed him the empty cup. He stared at it dumbly.

"That's a hell of a way to thank a man who's giving you a gig."

"I haven't seen a gig yet."

"Lucky you."

Meynard took a long drag of his cigarette. His hand was shaking. He was in a bad way. Welcome to the club.

The techs milled about the scene, snapping pictures and spreading powders and doing whatever it is that techs do. It was a good effort, but mostly wasteful. The Bugs had shut our databases down. Fingerprints were about as useful as toenail clippings. No national registry anymore, no feds to fax. But the cops had a file cabinet back at headquarters, and that cabinet had some local prints, and who knew? Maybe there'd be a match. Somebody has to win the lottery.

"What's the story?" I gestured toward the scene with my chin.

Meynard blew a thick cloud of smoke. "Go have a look for yourself."

I did. She was naked and pale and hideously exposed. She was huddled in the fetal position. She'd gone out of the world the same way she'd come in. And there hadn't been very long between those things.

She was a kid. Only a kid.

Now I understood why Meynard didn't want to talk about it.

Made in the USA
Columbia, SC
01 July 2019